Kissing A STRANGER

USA Today Bestselling Author

LACEY BLACK

Kissing A Stranger

The Kissing Games, book 4

Copyright © 2023 Lacey Black
Cover Design by The Book Cover Boutique
Photographer Wander Aguiar
Model Lucas Loyola

Editing by Kara Hildebrand
Proofreading by Sandra Shipman, Julie Deaton, Joanne Thompson, and Karen Hrdlicka
Format Design by Tami at Integrity Formatting

THE KISSING GAME SERIES

There are five books in the series.
Authors include: Molly McLain, Kaylee Ryan, C.A. Harms, Lacey Black, and Evan Grace.
All books can be read as standalone novels and can be read in any order.

Chapter ONE

Adeline

My phone vibrates.

Again.

I almost pull the device from my clutch and check the screen, but there's no need. I already know who's insistently texting me, despite the fact I took a long four-day weekend off from work to attend my oldest friend's big destination wedding in Florida. No one from the office would think to bother me right now, and it's not like I have a long list of close friends who'd be reaching out during such an important weekend.

Except one man.

My father.

He doesn't care, though, which is why I'm refusing to answer. I'll deal with the verbal lashing that'll result from my ignoring the messages later. Right now, I'm waiting for the wedding rehearsal to start. Actually, we're still waiting on the groom to arrive, but that's another story.

Audrey was one of my first friends in school. My father never tried to hide the fact he didn't approve, but I didn't care. We ran in different social circles, much to his dismay, but I think that's what I liked most about our friendship. She was nothing like the young girls my father preferred I hung out with. The ones from the country club or whose fathers dropped buckets of money on weekend shopping and spa trips for them. Audrey came from a regular, middle-class family, and I found over the years, I craved what she had. Hugs when she went off to school, ice cream sundaes in bed when her boyfriend broke up with her, seeing them in the stands at a sporting event or awards ceremony, and family meals around the dinner table every night.

At that point in my life, I couldn't remember when I shared a meal around the dining room table at home with both my parents. Only center table at the country club was suitable for the Montgomerys, where you could be seen. My father, the famed South Carolina defense attorney who shot to stardom by successfully getting the former governor of South Carolina off on money laundering and bribery charges, and my mother, a debutante with plenty of old-school money and a lifetime membership to said country club her granddaddy started. They were a match made in status-climbing heaven, and between their business schedules, never had time for their only daughter.

I was raised by Alma, my nanny, and Gladys, the housekeeper and cook. They made sure I did my homework, got the grades my parents expected of me, and taught me how to do more than just wait for others to wait on me hand and foot, the way my parents did. They're the real reason I didn't turn into a bitchy, entitled brat, the way so many of my "friends" did in school.

Everyone but Audrey. I clung to her like Saran Wrap, despite the fact my family didn't approve of our friendship.

Even though we went to different colleges after high school and grew slightly apart, she was always an anchor in my life, the slice of normalcy and stability I secretly yearned for, and that's why now, on her wedding weekend, I couldn't picture myself being anywhere else but by her side.

My phone vibrates again, and I have to bite my tongue not to express my displeasure at his persistence. I know nothing is wrong. I learned that lesson years ago. My father is used to getting his way, exactly when he wants it. People in the office bend over backward for him, doing anything and everything he could possibly ask, and unfortunately, that level of superiority includes me. He knows I'm busy. He's well aware of this weekend's schedule of events, but does he care?

No.

My jaw is clenched so tightly, I swear I could crack a molar, and since I can practically hear my mother in my ear telling me that's not ladylike, I force my face to relax and take a few deep, calming breaths.

"You okay?" Charlie asks.

I've always liked Charlie. She's Audrey's sister, older by two years, and was just as much a staple in my childhood as the younger Krause daughter. "I'm good. How's Audrey holding up?" I ask, easily switching the subject away from me.

The annoyance ebbs off Charlie in waves. "Starting to panic. We're fifteen minutes away from starting the rehearsal, and the groom is in another state."

I haven't been around Linc much since he started dating my oldest friend, he seems to work more than anyone I know, and considering I come from a workaholic father, that's saying something. I don't know him well enough to say whether I'm surprised by his absence or not, but I'm definitely not a fan of it. My friend is stressing, the worry evident in her pretty eyes.

"Come on, let's go over and try to keep her calm," I say, walking with Charlie to where Audrey and the other two bridesmaids, Lorelei and Amara, stand.

"Auds, you need to quit looking at your phone. It's only adding to your stress," Charlie says, taking Audrey's phone from her hand and passing it to Lorelei, who slips it into her purse.

"She's right," Lorelei replies. "And believe me when I say you're going to want to remember more about this weekend than waiting on messages. Try to enjoy as much of this as you can, Auds, even if Linc isn't here yet. You'll regret it if you don't."

Laughter can be heard moments before the groomsmen walk around the corner, joining us in the lobby. Audrey watches them approach, her eyes filling with tears. "Why are we even rehearsing? It's just silly without Linc."

Audrey's aunt Miranda, her only living relative, besides her sister, is right there. "Aw, sweetie. I'm sure one of the boys would be happy to stand in for him."

It seems a little odd to me, but what do I know? I've never been in a wedding before, let alone one where the groom is a no-show at the rehearsal. When Liam, the groom's younger brother, approaches and begins talking to Audrey, my phone vibrates once more in my purse. Sighing, I pull it from my clutch and see the name on the screen. "Excuse me. I'm going to make a quick call," I tell those around me before slipping off to the side of the group.

I know I shouldn't do this now, but I also realize he's going to keep texting and calling until I answer. Steeling my spine and taking a deep breath, I tap the call button and bring the device to my ear.

"Adeline."

"Good evening, Father. Is something wrong?" I know there isn't.

"You mean besides my only daughter ignoring my phone calls?"

Closing my eyes, I rub the spot beside my temple where the throb is starting. "I'm in the middle of Audrey's wedding rehearsal. Remember? I'm away for the weekend."

"Yes, yes, yes, of course I remember, but in case *you* forgot, this isn't a business where taking long weekends off is convenient nor appropriate right before a large trial."

I swallow over the lump in my throat. It's not like I'm on the trial team. Oh, no. My father doesn't want me too close to the action. Despite the fact I have a law degree like every other member of the Montgomery family going back three generations, he doesn't actually want me to use it. He'd prefer I be more seen, not heard, so I get stuck doing menial tasks like combing over data with the paralegals or retrieving his coffee like the assistants. This way, when he marries me off to the highest bidder—only slightly joking—he's not actually losing a prominent member of his team.

He's only losing me.

"It's not my fault Darian Fernando's trial got moved up two weeks." I leave out the reason why. The judge is taking a vacation, which is one of the reasons my father is so annoyed.

"Of course that's not your fault, but it doesn't help you're not here to assist. Everyone else is pulling your weight now, thanks to your little weekend trip to Florida."

"I'll be back in the office Monday morning," I reassure him for the umpteenth time.

"See that you are. We have much to go over before I'm needed in court."

"I'd be happy to accompany you," I add, even though I know that's fruitless too.

"Not necessary. We have it handled."

I close my eyes and will the tears away.

The truth is, I've never actually seen the inside of a courtroom since I graduated and took the bar exam. Daddy makes sure I'm only on small cases that settle outside of court. He says I need more experience, yet refuses to help me get it. I know it's part of his master plan, and the degree I hold is only for show. Once I meet the man of his dreams, I'll quit my job, bear grandchildren to carry on his legacy, and spend all my time fundraising for approved Montgomery charities.

My stomach knots at the thought.

"If you insist," I state, making sure to keep any and all emotion out of my words.

"I do. Now, let's talk about Jefferson Martin. He's agreed to have dinner with us Monday evening at Morticia's Steakhouse."

A wave of nausea hits full force, threatening to make my knees buckle. "Father," I start, but am cut off.

"His father will be attending as well, so I need you on your best behavior. If this relationship between you two is going to work, you need to stop sulking in the corner and act like you want to marry him."

I don't want to marry him!

"He's a catch," he continues, repeating Jefferson's attributes as if he's reading his dating profile. "His family and ours have been linked for generations. His grandfather started off as a partner with your grandfather until he was elected Attorney General for the state of South Carolina. Since then, Jefferson has been making a name for himself in our circle, becoming one of the most sought-after tax lawyers in Charleston."

I could repeat my father's spiel word for word at this point. I've heard it many times over in the last year, but despite his praises for Jefferson, I have no actual feelings for him, nor do I want to date him. He's not bad looking, with his designer suits and pristine, pressed white shirts. His hair is always salon-quality perfect and I'm certain he receives manicures at some point during the week because his nails are almost better than mine. His smile is warm, though it rarely reaches his eyes, and he's always polite and respectful.

And I feel absolutely nothing outside of a cordial acquaintanceship.

"We're meeting at seven. I expect you to be there. Wear that black Armani dress your mother had sent over to you last week."

I know better than to argue. "I'll be there," I reply, even though I'd rather be anywhere else.

"Good. Denise has already added it to your schedule," he states, making my heart drop in my chest. Denise is my assistant, who really doesn't do much assisting where I'm concerned. She works for my father and does exactly what he tells her to do. Any changes I make to my schedule, she'll go in and revert back to whatever it was he demanded.

"Fine."

"Be in the office at seven. I refuse to let you not pull your weight on this case or watch the ones you're on flounder and fall," he states before disconnecting the phone.

I close my eyes and take calming breaths. *Pull my weight*? I've been working sixty-plus hour weeks since I graduated from law school last spring. I put in more time than any of the junior associates and paralegals in the office, mostly because I don't want to be known as the daughter of one of the partners who doesn't do her fair share. I work my tail off, yet get absolutely none of the praise or acknowledgement for it.

Noticing the wedding party now gathering at the doors leading to the beach, I slip my phone back inside my clutch, refusing to think about the phone call. I'm here for my dearest friend, Audrey, and the last thing I want is to miss a single moment of her special weekend because my father is taking up headspace.

I step outside and listen to Wendy, the resort wedding planner, go through the details of tomorrow's big day. I'm walking with Liam, the groom's brother, who will also be standing in for said groom in his absence this evening. Liam appears to be more laidback than his brother and definitely has the good looks and fit body nailed down in the appearance department. I can see why my friend likes him so much. In fact, just watching Audrey and Liam from the outside, they give off the appearance that *they* could be the couple getting married tomorrow. They've always been such great friends, and you can feel that chemistry, fondness, and respect reflecting in their eyes.

My eyes are drawn to the other couples in the wedding party. Charlie is Audrey's sister and maid of honor, while Spencer is the best man. I don't know a lot of the history between those two, but they appear to be at odds with one another every chance they get. I know they went to college together and somewhere along the way formed a rivalry that has continued to this day.

Jasper and Lorelei are married. Jasper was friends with Linc and Liam when they were younger and reconnected with the older brother during college. I'm told he's a large animal vet. His wife, Lorelei, works with Audrey at Magnolia Marketing, and introduced the happy couple at a party a few years back.

Rounding out the wedding party is Ty and Amara. They're not dating, but every once in a while, I catch a hint of interest in their eyes when they think the other isn't looking. He's a fireman and EMT by day and appears to have a wild streak a mile long. Amara is an absolute sweetheart and recently opened her own hair salon and day spa. She's tasked with hair and makeup for tomorrow's big day.

When we've completed two run-throughs, we're released to one of the smaller rooms for the rehearsal dinner. It's called the Seaside Room for good reason, with its breathtaking views of the ocean, it's one of the many charming qualities of Belisa Beach Resort. This place is nestled on Florida's east coast and provides spectacular views and top-notch amenities. I can see why Audrey chose this location for her destination wedding.

We all start to file into the room, while Audrey pauses in the hallway to make a call. "You've got this, girl," I tell my friend, rubbing her back.

"I know," she replies, trying to give me a look of confidence, but I see the fear and worry hidden in her eyes. I can't imagine my husband-to-be not showing up when expected for our wedding.

My thoughts immediately turn to Jefferson. I can't marry a man I don't love. I won't. Even if he was hand chosen by my father, I know there's only one real reason for him to push us together. My father has political dreams of his own, and having your daughter married to the governor's son would certainly help give you the right connections to make those dreams come to fruition.

But I refuse to think about him now.

Heading for the long table in the room, my feet stumble when my eyes land on the man behind the private bar. He's...wow. Strikingly gorgeous in a way I've never found attractive before. His dark hair looks stylishly wind tussled and his stunning brown eyes gleam with mischief and dirty promises. He's wearing a well-fitted dress shirt with the sleeves rolled up, exposing corded muscles and a dark tattoo. My father always hates it when men roll up their sleeves, saying it diminished the sophistication and seriousness the suit provided, but I have to admit, right now, I've never seen a dress shirt look so good.

This man is nothing like the ones I usually find myself attracted to, yet the moment he looks up and meets my gaze, I feel more electricity and desire running through my veins than I ever have before, and I can't seem to pull my eyes away from him.

"Ready?" Charlie asks, slipping her arm inside mine and forcing me to walk toward the bar. There's a short line, as the others in the wedding party grab drinks, and when it's finally our turn at the bar, we step up to place our order.

"Ladies, good evening. What can I get you to drink?" the sexy man croons in a deep, husky voice that does inappropriate things between my thighs.

"Beer for me," Charlie replies.

I'm not a fan of beer, so I opt for my tried-and-true, go-to drink. "Watermelon martini, please."

The man smiles. "Coming right up, beautiful."

I can feel Charlie's smirk but keep my eyes trained elsewhere so I don't have to answer the questions she's ready to ask. Unable to stop myself, I glance at the man behind the bar, who's making my drink. Only his eyes aren't on his task. They're on me.

I slip a tip into the jar as he places my glass in front of me. "Thank you," I say, proud of myself for keeping my voice even and not giving away the sudden wave of nervousness I feel.

He nods, offering me a confident smile as I turn to walk away. "Umm, hello, gorgeous," Charlie whispers, sipping her beer as we go.

"He's all right," I mutter, hating how easy it was to lie to her, because he was way more than all right. He was gorgeous.

Stunning.

Like the love child of Chris Hemsworth and Ryan Reynolds.

We enjoy a delicious meal and chat, and I don't say much, but that's typical for me. I enjoy sitting back and watching those around me, and with this group, there's plenty to see. There's an easiness to their friendships, a hint of humor in their bickering, and I have to admit, I'm a little envious. I have friends back home in Charleston, but none that I consider *real*. Sure they'd have no problem telling me the dress I was wearing didn't flatter my tall five-ten frame or the way I had my blond hair styled was so last season, but they aren't people I can call to discuss things going on in my life.

I also steal many glances at the bartender. I haven't caught his name yet, but I have caught his eyes on me plenty. Each time, it's like a caress. One that starts at my neck and works its way down my abdomen to my under-used lady bits.

Maybe in another time I could find the bravery to approach him. I've never had to make the first move before, but the very thought of walking up to him and striking up a flirty conversation sets my soul on fire with wonder and excitement. Perhaps a few more drinks, and I'll be willing to take the chance.

To be the woman I dream of being.

To be free.

Chapter TWO

Decker

She's absolutely stunning.

There's something magnificent about the blond woman sitting at the table, enjoying a meal with her friends. I've been watching her since the moment she walked into the private room. I was aware of her long legs as she approached the bar to order a drink, and I'm even more aware of them now that I catch peeks beneath the table. She's tall, probably only a couple of inches shorter than my six-foot frame, and has the most alluring blue eyes I've ever seen.

She also screams money. I've been around plenty of women in my line of work to know who has it and who wishes they did. From her designer summer dress to the sandals on her feet, expensive manicure, and pedicure, expertly styled hair and makeup, and diamonds in her ears big enough to feed a third world country, she has a lot more money wrapped up in her appearance than the other women at the table. Not that it's a bad thing, just that she sticks out a little more because of it.

If I had to speculate, I'd say family money. She doesn't wear a wedding ring, so my guess is not a trophy wife. Though, I've also learned at this job that wearing a ring isn't always the telltale sign of a spouse. I've met several women on weekend girls' trips here who don't wear a ring and still want to play. Those are the ones who are more trouble than any other woman you encounter. She's also not sitting directly beside a guy in the wedding party. None of them are staring at her like she hung the moon and the stars, so I'm guessing she's not dating anyone in the group.

Lucky me.

When the dinner plates are cleared away, a few from the group get up and head in my direction. I get drinks quickly, keeping the alcohol flowing, especially for the bride. What I notice almost immediately is the absence of a groom. I've overheard bits and pieces of conversations and learned the groom is still in their home state of South Carolina, tied up with work. I hate to be the one to break it to them, but usually if someone hasn't arrived by this point of the wedding weekend, there's a damn good chance they're not coming at all.

I've seen only a couple of canceled weddings in my time here. A runaway bride was my first one, while a groom fucking the best man was the cause of the second. Yes, the best man. They were caught enjoying a little pre-wedding head in the honeymoon suite just an hour before the I do's. Who caught them? The bride's mother.

Epic blow-up.

Especially since the groom repeatedly insisted he was just blowing off steam.

The staff still talks about the drama that unfolded as a result.

But a few months back, we had a bride who was late to the rehearsal. The poor groom was sweating buckets, making excuse after excuse as to why she wasn't down there yet. When they finally got her to the rehearsal, she had that look in her eye that screamed runner and kept staring out at the ocean as if it held all the answers to life's problems.

Well, I think it did hold her answers, because sometime later that night, she snuck out of the resort, chartered a boat, and took off for the Bahamas. The guy had been devastated the next morning when he got the news, much like I imagine this bride will be tomorrow. I'd throw a Benjamin on the bar that says I'm right. Sadly, all the signs are there, even though I hope I'm wrong.

I consider myself an expert at reading people. It's part of my job. From the time I stepped behind my first bar at twenty-one to now, I've learned how to be effective at what I do. I chat with the lonely, keep the liquor flowing for the lively, and on occasion, offer a piece of advice or two. I've even taken up a handful of ladies on what they have to offer at the end of the night.

Though, not at the same time.

I like women, but I'm not a complete douchebag.

As the evening progresses, the older couple, as well as another older lady say goodbye to the group. I'm assuming they're the parents of the happy couple, one of which is still not present for the evening. As they exit the room, the gorgeous blonde approaches with an empty glass.

"Another?" I ask, reaching for her dirty glass.

"Yes, please."

I set out to make her another watermelon martini, retrieving a fresh glass, vodka, and watermelon juice. As I pour all the ingredients in the shaker, I glance her direction and ask, "So, are you family or friend of the happy couple?"

"Friend," she replies, glancing over her shoulder to where the bride sits, drinking. "Audrey, the bride, and I are old school friends."

Nodding, I pour the sweet concoction into the glass and reach for the small wedges of watermelon, garnishing the drink with a slice of fruit. "One of my finest watermelon martinis," I boast, placing the drink in front of her.

She smiles, the gesture lighting up her entire face. "Thank you. I'd never had one before until I came here. I usually stick with dirty martinis with extra olives."

A wicked smile spreads across my lips. "Ahh, a dirty girl. I like it."

The beauty is taking a sip of her drink and practically chokes on it. She covers her mouth as she mutters, "Well, I don't know about that."

Leaning against the bar, I ask, "So, dirty girl, what's your name?"

"Adeline."

I extend my hand. "Decker. It's nice to meet you, Adeline." The moment she places her delicate hand inside mine, electricity rushes through my veins. My balls start to tingle, which is crazy, because I've never had this kind of reaction to a woman based solely on a touch.

Clearing my throat, I rest my elbows in front of me, giving her my full attention. "So, Adeline, how are you enjoying our beautiful resort?"

Her eyes sparkle with excitement. "It's beautiful. We're in one of the suites, which works perfectly for our small group."

"Have you enjoyed the pool or beach access yet?" I ask, trying not to picture her in a bikini but failing miserably.

"Not yet. We did a spa day yesterday, and that was amazing."

Leaning in even more, I catch a whiff of her floral scent. It makes my dick stand up and take notice too. "The spa, huh? Like manis and pedis?"

"Of course," she replies, taking another sip of her martini. "Plus massages and facials. It was heavenly."

"I've heard good things about the spa, but I've never been. It weirds me out having someone rubbing around on my feet," I confess, doing anything I can to keep her talking.

"Really? Foot massage phobia?"

"More like pink sparkly toenail polish phobia."

She giggles the sweetest sound, and I've never been more addicted to something in my life. "You don't have to get them painted."

"I'm not taking my chances. I took the last donut one day in the employee break room and Hilga wasn't happy with me. She might paint them just for spite."

"Nail polish revenge? Bold move," she replies, swirling the liquid in her glass before taking another small sip. "What if it was something a little more manly?"

"Like green sparkly nail polish?" I quip.

Throwing her head back, she laughs hard at my question. Her slender neck is on display, begging for my mouth, my tongue. I can picture it now, my hands sliding into her hair, my lips caressing that soft column of skin until she's whimpering and begging for more. "Green is definitely a possibility," I agree, leaning in until my mouth is dangerously close to hers. "But I was thinking more of a blue so it matches your eyes, because they are, without a doubt, the most stunning shade of sapphire I've ever seen."

A blush creeps up her neck from her chest, making the soft yellows and pinks of her sundress that much more vibrant. "Thank you," she whispers, looking at me from beneath her eyelashes.

I open my mouth, ready to ask her...for something. A date? A drink after I get off work? To run away with me to a foreign country? Hell, I don't know. I just want more time, I guess, but unfortunately, that doesn't appear to be in the cards tonight. She offers me a small, private smile and says, "I should probably get back over to my friends."

Nodding, I reach for a towel and wipe off the top of the bar. "Well, you know where I am if you need another drink."

Soft pink lips curl upward. "I do. Thank you, Decker."

"Anytime, Adeline," I reply, my heartbeat kicking up a few extra beats the second she turns to walk away.

I watch her and the group for a while, refilling drinks and chatting with those who approach the bar. Not too long later, the bride checks her phone. "Anyway, it's getting late, and I have a big day ahead of me tomorrow."

The room erupts with celebration.

The guys all announce they're staying behind, waiting on the groom, and I can't help but smile when I hear Adeline add, "I might hang out with the guys for a bit." She looks up, our eyes meeting from across the room.

The bride, a little wobbly on her feet, leans in and says something to her, but I can't hear it over the rest of the chatting. I hang back and try to keep myself busy as the ladies all head out of the room, leaving behind four guys and Adeline. The five remaining members of the wedding party head to the bar.

The guys order a round of shots, including one for Adeline. She makes a face when the best man sets the glass of amber liquid in front of her. "What's that?" she asks, her eyes zeroed in on the alcohol.

"Tequila. The good stuff," the man his friends call Spencer says.

"Uhh," she replies with a shutter. "I'm going to need the salt and lime."

I place the requests in front of her, adding, "It's smooth, Addi. You really don't need it."

She meets my gaze, clearly not sure she can trust me. "I doubt it. The last time I did a shot of tequila was in college, and it was vile."

"That's because it was cheap. Good tequila doesn't require salt and lime, but if it'll make you feel better, I've got you," I add, sliding the saltshaker even closer.

"Come on, Adeline! Shots!" one of the other guys bellows, holding his glass in the air. "To Linc and Audrey. May their day go off without a hitch."

"Cheers," the rest reply, tapping glasses and downing their shots of liquid.

Adeline licks her hand, that pink tongue dancing across her tanned skin like foreplay, and shakes a touch of salt in its wake. Then, she drags her tongue across the salted skin and brings the shot glass to her lips. My dick is definitely hard watching the display, especially when she grabs the lime wedge and sucks.

"Yeah!" the guys cheer, replacing their empty glasses onto the bar.

Once they start talking again, I turn my full attention to Adeline. "Not so bad, was it?"

She shakes her head. "It wasn't."

"I told you. The good tequila isn't bad at all. Velvety smooth and full of flavor."

Her eyes drop to my mouth, and I can't help but wonder if she's thinking about my lips the way I'm thinking about hers. Just like the alcohol, they appear silky smooth, and I'm dying for one little taste.

Clearing her throat, she shakes her head slightly before reaching for her drink. It's almost empty, which pleases me. That means she's going to need to hang around a bit longer while I make her another. "You called me Addi."

Tossing a dry towel over my shoulder, I cross my arms and lean back against the small cooler behind me. "I did."

"No one calls me Addi," she whispers, almost absently.

"No? Adeline is a beautiful name, but the nickname seemed to be suitable for the situation."

"I liked it," she replies quickly, her eyes a bit wide when she looks up at me. "My family is fairly formal. They always use my full given name."

I move closer, suddenly needing to crowd her personal space as I ask, "What do you prefer? Adeline? Or Addi?"

She doesn't answer right away, which makes me wonder if I somehow crossed the line. This woman is clearly out of my league, and maybe she's realizing it now too. I'm just a bartender with no post-high school education. I've bounced around from job to job, town to town. Hell, even state to state since the day I left home at twenty-three. For seven years, I've been a nomad, living my life under my terms.

"Addi."

Her response surprises me, and I'm unable to keep that shock off my face. "Yeah?"

She shrugs. "It sounds nice coming from your lips," she states, slowly bringing her glass to her own lips and emptying the contents.

Elbows on the bar, I bring my mouth to her ear and whisper, "How about Adeline when others are around, but Addi when it's just you and me?"

Her throat bobs as she swallows, a shiver sweeps through her body. My eyes rake across her bare shoulders and down her arms as goose bumps prickle her skin. "Deal."

A slow, sultry smile spreads across her mouth. I don't know why this feels like such a big victory, but it does. Maybe because this incredibly gorgeous woman is still talking to me and isn't outwardly flirting. She's making me work for it, but that hesitation doesn't feel like a game. It's genuine, as if she's perhaps not used to having someone shower her with praise and attention, but that can't be right. This woman is fucking gorgeous. Surely she has men falling at her feet on a daily basis.

As the night wears on, the guys become drunker, while Adeline switches to water. They try to engage her in conversation, but she seems content just to sit back and watch. A few times, she takes her phone out of her small purse and a scowl spreads across her face. She even gasps, her delicate fingers covering her mouth as she stares down at the device. Whatever she's reading irritates her, but she never says a word to any of the guys or me.

When the clock nears midnight, she gets up from where she sits and heads my way, placing her empty water glass on the counter. "Another?" I ask, hoping she's not ready to call it a night, but knowing what's about to come out of her mouth.

"No, thank you, I'm going to turn in for the night."

I take her glass and place it to the side to wash. "Too bad."

"Thank you for the drinks." Her eyes meet mine as she adds, "And the company."

"You're most welcome, beautiful Addi," I reply, resorting to the private nickname I've given her. "Do you need to be escorted up to your suite?"

She shakes her head immediately. "No, I'm okay. I stopped drinking a while ago."

Nodding, I reach out and place my hand on hers. "It's been a pleasure."

Again, she blushes the faintest shade of pink. "Likewise." She starts to turn away, my hand still cupping hers, but pauses. "Perhaps I'll get to see you again before I leave Sunday."

My cock kicks in my dress slacks, clearly hoping he's invited to the party. "Perhaps," I reply casually, even though I want to agree right away.

I release her hand and watch her walk away, my eyes glued to the sway of her ass as her long, shapely legs carry her out of the private room and out of sight. "Damn," I mutter.

"How's it going?"

I turn to find Janine approaching, that ever-present serious scowl on her face. "Good."

The bar manager turns her attention to the four guys still sitting at the table, laughing and joking as they continue to drink. "They doing okay?"

"Appear to be," I reply.

"Listen, I know you're off tomorrow night, but Julio went home sick. I'm pretty certain he won't be well enough to work tomorrow, and with the wedding, I don't want to take any chances at being understaffed. Are you available to work?"

"Sure," I agree instantly, knowing Adeline will still be here for the wedding, giving me another opportunity to see her.

"Thank you. I've got you in the bar with Shana," Janine informs me.

Disappointment fills my chest. If I'm in the bar, that means I won't be able to see and talk to Adeline at the reception. "Sounds good," I state, even though it feels anything but.

She nods before turning and exiting the room, leaving me alone with the remaining wedding party.

Just after one, someone notes the fact the groom hasn't arrived yet, and by two thirty, it's time for me to close down the private bar. I'm not sure if they're irritated with me for ending their night of drinking or at the no-show, but the four men are not happy. When the man I now know as Liam, the groom's brother, says, "Fucking Linc," I realize their frustration isn't directed at me, but at the missing groom.

I hate to be the one to tell them, but that groom isn't coming.

They'll discover that fact as soon as their liquor wears off. This wedding isn't going to happen. I feel it in my bones.

Now, what will that mean for beautiful Adeline?

I wonder if our time will be cut too short, or if perhaps it gives me a little more time to get to know her. Either way, she'll be heading home at some point, and I'll remain here.

Might as well make the most of it while I can.

Chapter THREE

Adeline

"I can't believe today is the day." Amara smiles across the breakfast table at Audrey, who has been grinning from the moment she woke up.

"It was really sweet of your family to come, by the way," the bride states. I learned Amara is also Linc and Liam's cousin, so today's marriage officially makes the two women family too. I love that for Audrey. She was in high school when her parents were killed in a car accident, and I know it really affected her. Still does. She and Charlie went to live with their only living relative, Aunt Miranda, and has always craved deep connections and family since.

"They wouldn't miss this for the world," Amara says. "Besides, my mom is always looking for a reason to road trip."

"Speaking of which," I start, trying to speak over my suddenly dry throat. "I kinda wish I'd brought my own car."

Charlie frowns as she chews. "Why?" she asks, knowing I rode to Florida with her and the bride.

I hold her gaze, trying not to show my anxiety as I recall the text messages I received late last night from my father. I refuse to allow his behavior to tarnish today's celebration. I casually shrug my shoulders and say, "I think I want to stay a bit longer."

No way can I go home right now.

Not when I'd be walking straight into the lion's den.

Lorelei lifts her brows curiously. "Don't tell me it's because of the bartender."

Before she can finish her statement, I'm shaking my head. "His name is Decker, and no. It isn't because of him. I just like it here, and I'm not ready to go home."

I don't tell them why.

"What is your dad on your back about now?" Amara asks, clearly understanding my family dynamics, despite only knowing me a brief time.

"What *isn't* he on my back about?" I ask, taking a hearty bite of my pancakes. I don't usually eat such sugary breakfast foods, but since my life seemed to implode spectacularly late last night, I figured I was due. "Anyway," I say, trying to chew and swallow, "I might stay. Sorry, Charlie, but you'll be going home alone."

"Story of my life," the maid of honor replies, making us all giggle.

Once breakfast is complete, the real fun begins. Hair and makeup commence, with Amara taking the lead, since she's the hairdresser of the group. Charlie and Lorelei help keep the mimosas flowing, and the mood is so light and jovial. We're literally having the best time getting ready, and even though this group is technically Audrey's friends, I'm having a wonderful time with them.

A knock at the door echoes through the suite, and Amara is the first one to head in that direction. "Should I make sure it's not Linc?" she calls out.

"He knows better," Audrey states, making us all giggle. Tradition states it's bad luck to see the bride before the wedding, which is why we've remained in our suite all morning, including having breakfast and mimosas delivered.

"Ohh, it's the other West brother," she says with one eye over the peephole. "And he brought his friends."

She swings the door open, and the moment I see their faces I know something's terribly wrong. My stomach clenches as Liam approaches Audrey, who gets to her feet right away, clearly seeing the distress on their faces. "What's wrong?" she asks.

"You should sit down, Audrey," Liam says carefully, and that's when I know.

Linc isn't coming.

Blood swooshes in my ears as I watch the groom's brother tell my oldest friend that her husband-to-be isn't here. That the wedding they've spent months planning isn't happening.

"Oh my God." Audrey loses it, and Liam pulls her into his arms to console her.

I'm unable to stop my own tears as I watch my friend cry, her gut-wrenching sobs filling the suite. Charlie goes over and pulls her into her own embrace, hugging her sister to her chest and together, they cry. I leave long enough to grab the box of Kleenex from the bathroom and place it on the couch. The guys, all with crestfallen faces, are leaving, heading out to deliver the devastating news to the wedding planner and the family who traveled three states to get here for this weekend.

The moment the door shuts, Lorelei wraps her arms around Audrey. "I am so sorry, Auds. What can we do? Do you want to go home and kick his ass?"

Amara snorts and nods her head. "I'm down for that."

"Me too," I decide, even though I'm the least confrontational person on the planet.

"I don't want to see him," Audrey insists. "Can I get a drink? Without the orange juice this time?"

"Absolutely." I practically sprint over to the kitchen area to get my friend a glass of champagne.

"You sure that's a good idea?" Charlie asks when I hand over the drink, a frown marring her face. "We have a lot to figure out."

"No, we don't," Audrey insists, taking a hearty drink. "I'm done worrying about the mess he's caused."

Lorelei hugs her friend. "Oh, sweetie. I hate this for you."

We all do.

What are we supposed to do now?

As the sun begins to set, Audrey goes to the honeymoon suite for a little peace and quiet, and honestly, I don't blame her. If I were walking in her shoes right now, I'd want to be alone too to wallow in my misery. I can't believe we're at this point. We should be at the reception, watching the happy couple dance their first dance. Instead, the bride is single, sporting puffy eyes from crying, and drinking herself into a stupor in the suite she should be sharing with her new husband.

What a mess.

My phone vibrates once more. "You've got to be kidding me," I mutter, floored he has the audacity to contact me right now. Not just because of where I'm at, though that should be reason enough for him to not contact me right now. As far as he knows, my best friend got married today, and I'm helping her celebrate. Yet, here he is, texting and calling me, as if he didn't just crush me under his designer leather shoes last night with a single company email.

"Your dad?" Charlie asks from her seat at the table. I can't help but notice how close Spencer is, but if she notices, she's not pointing it out.

Nodding, I mutter, "Who else."

Just then, Decker walks over, a smile on his sexy face. He's been behind the bar since we decided to come down and drink away our problems, but besides a cordial greeting, we haven't been able to talk much.

He places his hands on the back of my chair, and I have to tilt my head back to see him. Deciding to give him my full attention, thanks to a little liquid courage running through my veins, I flip my phone down so no one can see my screen and offer a smile. "How's it going?" he asks with his own flirty grin.

I feel my cheeks flush a bit, but I'm going to chalk it up to the alcohol we're drinking and not the fact he's standing extremely close, and I can smell his delicious cologne. It's woodsy and rich and makes my thighs clench just a little tighter.

"Good," Charlie replies, as I nod in agreement, my tongue thick and dry.

"Can I get you all anything?" he asks, his thumb sliding gently over my bare shoulder and making me shiver. The same thing happened last night when we touched. It just...does things to me.

Charlie drains her glass, her fruity concoction now gone. "I need a refill, but I'll follow you to the bar. Adeline?"

I still have half a glass of the strawberry drink, so I wave her off. "I'm good. Thank you."

She gets up, and I grin when I notice Spencer does the same. "I'll come with you," he says, following behind her as she heads to the bar.

Decker glances over his shoulder. "We'll talk soon."

Nodding, I sit back at the table and people-watch. Charlie and Spencer are at the bar. The sexual tension coming off them is enough to get a woman who is standing too close pregnant. Jasper and Lorelei are dancing, and the sadness ebbing from them is stifling. I don't know what's going on with them, nor am I close enough of a friend to ask, but clearly, they're dealing with a private issue. And Ty and Amara have since disappeared. I've caught enough while sharing a suite with these ladies to know Amara has a big crush on Ty, and I hope their absence means something where their attraction is concerned.

Then there's me. Since Liam is a no-show, I'm going to assume he's up with Audrey. She wanted to be alone, but something tells me she'd welcome him into the suite without so much as a second-guess. They're friends, yes, but I can't help but wonder if there's possibly more there. The way he looked at her during the rehearsal was the exact way his brother should have been looking at the bride as she made her way toward him.

I guess time will tell how the cards fall where they're concerned.

I sip what's left of my fruity concoction in my glass. One of the pluses about staying at this amazing beach resort is the drinks. They have a different set of specials every day, and each one has been positively delicious. I figured, while I was enjoying myself away from home, I might as well step out of my comfort zone and take advantage of all the resort has to offer.

In fact, I've already reserved a new room. Not that I don't want to stay with the rest of the wedding party, I know they're all going their separate ways tomorrow morning, and I've decided to stay. My father is going to be fuming mad when I tell him, but that's okay. I'm fuming mad at the email I was sent late last night and have had to swallow that anger with each reply I've seen from my fellow colleagues.

Realizing my drink is about empty, I slowly rise from my seat and decide to move to the bar. There's no need for me to take up a bigger table when I'm the last one there. Besides, finding an empty seat at the end of the bar allows me to watch Decker for a while. He's wearing black dress slacks again, with a white button-down shirt. Even though the blue tie is wrapped perfectly around his neck, the sleeves are rolled up once more, giving me a delicious view of the black ink.

When he spots me taking the available seat, he offers me a sexy smile and heads my way. "You look like you could use another drink."

The alcohol is freely flowing through my veins, but I'm not intoxicated. I've taken it slow enough to ensure I'm not drunk. Unlike Charlie, who is a little tipsy as she leaves the bar with Spencer. I can't help but smile at their retreating backs. I hope they quit fighting whatever it is they're fighting, and just finish that kiss they just shared.

"I think I could use another," I tell the man before me, tipping my empty glass. "And possibly some more food."

Decker reaches beneath the bar and grabs a menu. "How hungry are you?"

"Not starving, but I definitely need a little food in my stomach."

"Then try either the blooming onion or the zesty bacon-wrapped shrimp. Both are top selling appetizers and would be enough for a small meal," he advises, placing the menu on the bar so I can see the list of appetizers.

Scanning the options, my eyes settle on the shrimp. "How spicy are the shrimp?" I ask, noting the jalapeno.

"Not bad at all. They're minced and mixed with the cream cheese. It's a large fresh shrimp, split down the middle with the jalapeno and cream cheese mixture stuffed inside. Then, it's wrapped in bacon, grilled to perfection, and served with a homemade zesty dipping sauce."

"Okay, I do admit, that sounds delicious."

His smile makes my breath catch in my throat. "They're my favorite."

Nodding, I slide the menu back to him. "I'll take that. And maybe a small garden salad with the raspberry vinaigrette dressing."

"Coming right up," he replies with a wink before heading over to the computer system to put in my order. When his task is complete, he points to my drink. "Another?"

"Maybe just water until I eat a little food."

Again, he grins, and it's the sexiest thing I've ever seen in person. How can one man's smile be so beautiful, so heart-stopping? "Coming right up, beautiful." He fills a glass with ice, his eyes never leaving me for very long. Somehow, he fills a drink while barely looking at it, and makes it look easy at the same time. "The best iced water this side of the coast," he quips, presenting the water to me like it's a prize and bringing my own smile to my lips.

"Thank you, kind sir."

He glances to his right and says, "Give me a moment. I'll be back."

I watch as he moves down the bar and fills a drink order for a couple who are clearly on their honeymoon. A pang hits me square in the chest as I try to subtly watch them cuddle with each other. The love they share is still so vibrant and electrifying, you can't help but smile and pull for them.

My mind drifts to my friend in the fancy suite situated high above us. Audrey has the breathtaking view and the fancy room but lacks the other half of her soul to share it with. For some time, I assumed that person was Linc, but unfortunately, that turned out to be false.

What would it be like to actually find your person? The one who complements you in every way, who stands by your side, and truly listens to your wants and needs. Every person I've ever dated has been at the insistence of my father. A boy from the country club took me to prom. The son of one of the law firm partners dated me in college. A young man with strong political ties to the life my father wants for himself was offered my virginity at twenty, took it, and then moved on to the next girl who could help elevate his status.

No one I've ever dated has been with me for *me*, and that thought is gut-wrenching, especially because I'm well aware of the real reasons Jefferson Martin is being presented to me on a silver platter. Not because he might actually love me one day and make me happy, but because of what he could do for my family.

For my father.

"Penny for your thoughts?"

I look up and offer a sad grin to the man leaning against the bar in front of me. He has delivered my salad, and I was so lost in my own thoughts, I didn't even notice. "I'm sorry, I was just thinking," I say, brushing off his question. There is no way he wants to actually know what's going through my mind right now, and I refuse to give my father any more real estate there. Pouring the dressing over my salad, I lean in and ask, "Honeymoon couple?"

He doesn't even look in the direction of the couple, who are practically making out at the bar. "Yep. Tonight's their last night here. I believe they checked in last Sunday and will be heading home to somewhere in Illinois."

"Illinois. I've never been," I state unnecessarily.

"Me either, but it's on the list."

Stabbing a small piece of lettuce with my fork, I bring it to my mouth and ask, "There's a list?"

His eyes brighten as he grins. "There's definitely a list. You don't have one?"

"Of places I'd like to go?"

He nods, watching my mouth intently as I take a bite of my food and slowly chew. "Yeah."

"You first," I reply, bringing my hand to cover my mouth as I swallow.

"Locally, Oahu, Alaska, Illinois—I want to attend a Cubs game and see Navy Pier—Mount Rushmore and the Black Hills, and Northern California. I want to camp amongst the giant redwoods. Internationally, Bali, Portugal, and Italy are on my travel bucket list."

"I've been to Hawaii, but not Oahu. I'd love to visit Pearl Harbor," I confess, always having a secret love for history. When we visited the Hawaiian Islands, it was strictly part of a shopping tropical vacation at a resort. Mother wouldn't visit anywhere historical if her life depended on it.

"Me too. And I've always loved the history behind Wrigley Field, which is why I'd love to see a game there sometime."

I mentally run through his list, and realize many are beautiful, historical landmarks. "I didn't peg you for a history buff," I state, taking another small bite of my salad.

"Ehh, not so much a history buff as I enjoy seeing beautiful, unique places, many of which tell a story about where we all came from and how we got to where we are."

I nod, understanding and appreciating his perspective. "Favorite place you've seen so far?"

"Belisa Beach Resort," he replies instantly. "The view is as stunning as the ocean outside the door."

Is he talking about me?

I blink, my mouth falling open in a very unladylike way. Thank God I didn't have food in my mouth, or it was liable to horrifyingly fall out onto my lap.

Winking, he stands up straight and taps the bar. "I'll be right back with the rest of your food."

My eyes trail him until he disappears around the corner, and I'm left a little flustered and a bit turned on at the same time. He's definitely flirting with me, but I'm just not certain what to do about it. He probably flirts with everyone, honestly. Decker has that outgoing type of personality.

Yet, I can't stop thinking about the fact I'm in another state, far away from the prying eyes and life I'm forced to lead. What would happen if, just for one single night, I did what *I* wanted to do? What if I left all the pretenses, the drama, and the unhappiness behind, and just enjoyed a little me-time at this small, private resort without the world watching?

Am I bold enough to flat out ask for the things floating through my mind?

A smile crosses my lips as I wonder if Decker would be interested in helping a girl forget about her life for a night.

Two nights, tops.

Chapter FOUR

Decker

Something's up with Adeline. She's different since she ate her dinner. Calmer, maybe? Relaxed, even? As if the invisible weight she was carrying on her shoulders suddenly disappeared. And it's not the alcohol talking either. She hasn't drunk enough to classify as inebriated, or even happily buzzed for that matter, but there is definitely a fire dancing in her gorgeous blue eyes as she watches me.

And hell, has she been watching me. Every move I make, I feel her eyes follow. I know this because I can't seem to take my eyes off her either.

"I think you have an admirer," Shana states with a smirk, her gaze over my shoulder to the end of the bar where Adeline sits.

"You think?" I ask, not giving her anything.

"Oh, for sure. Play your cards right, and you'll be slipped a keycard before the end of the night." Shana slaps me on the back before moving down to the far end of the bar to help a customer.

I glance back at Adeline, who offers me a small smile. Turning, I head in her direction, grateful it's nearing the end of the night and the bar is not very crowded. "Ready for another?" I ask, nodding toward her water. She switched to H2O more than an hour ago.

She shakes her head. "I'm good, thank you. I'd like to pay my tab," she says, pulling a small wallet from the thin purse on the bar.

Disappointment settles in my gut, but I don't let it show. I have another thirty minutes left of work, grateful to be nearing the end of my shift, but a little disheartened I'll be parting ways with Adeline, probably for good. "Coming right up," I reply, taking her offered card and walking over to the computer system to bring up her tab. I run the card and print the slip for her to sign.

She scrawls her name across the line and adds a generous tip to the total before sliding it back toward me. "Thank you," she says, slipping her credit card back inside the small purse.

"You're very welcome." I want to say more, but what? She's leaving sometime tomorrow—or today, since it's after midnight.

She slowly slides from the barstool and stands, slipping the purse under her arm. A strong resolve fills her eyes as she straightens her back and meets my gaze head-on. "Listen, I don't know what time you get off work, but I'm not really ready to go to bed. I thought about going for a walk on the beach and watching the ocean for a while."

I have to fight the smile threatening to spread across my lips. "I'm off in about thirty minutes actually."

Her eyes sparkle as she asks, "Care to join me?"

My cock kicks in my slacks with eagerness. "I'd love to," I reply honestly, grateful for the chance to spend a few more hours with her.

"Great. Where should we meet?"

"How about outside the main entrance by the cobblestone walk-way," I suggest.

Adeline nods in agreement. "I'll see you there," she says, turning and walking out of the bar with her head held high. She pays no attention to the three guys at a small table off to the side who all turn and watch her leave, no doubt staring at her ass as she goes. It's a sight to behold in her sexy summer dress.

After twenty long minutes, Shana stops beside me. "Go."

"What?" I ask, glancing around the room to see there's only four patrons left. The three guys at the table and a lone man at the bar.

"I can handle it until close. Besides, you're only leaving ten minutes early anyway. Go. Meet up with that woman."

My eyebrows draw together in question. "I don't know what you're talking about."

She barks out a laugh. "Riiiiight. I think I saw her outside by the beach about five minutes ago. If you hurry, you can catch her."

I don't tell my co-worker I already have plans to meet up with her. It's none of her business, but I'm also not going to look a gift horse in the mouth if I have the opportunity to steal a little extra time with her. "I'll go, but only because it's dead and has been for a while."

She shrugs. "The cancellation of the wedding definitely put a damper on the night."

She's not wrong. Usually, on event nights, we're much busier. Between the live music and the happy, wedding vibes, people tend to congregate at the bar longer than nights without it. "I'll see you Tuesday night," I tell her, reaching for the computer to clock out.

"I'm on tomorrow night, but off a few days after that," she tells me, being polite.

"Enjoy your free time," I tell her, taking my share of the tips and slipping the cash into my pocket.

"You too," she replies, a knowing grin on her pretty face.

I keep my pace even as I head out, detouring when I exit the bar and making my way to the front entrance instead of the back one used by employees. The overnight reception clerk is there and offers me a nod as I pass, moving out of the automatic sliding doors and into the warm, summer night.

My eyes scan the walkway from left to right, a wild extra beat in my heart kicks in the moment I spot her down on the beach. She's staring out at the water, her sandals hanging from her fingers as her hair and the skirt of her dress blows in the breeze. She's positively breathtaking.

I don't know how long I stand here, watching, but it's both not long enough and too long. Every second I wait to go to her is a second I lose, because she's taking off tomorrow. With determined strides, I make my way to where she stands on the beach. I spot a couple down a ways, holding hands and walking in the surf, but no one else is around.

The moment I step into the sand, I realize my mistake. No way can I walk in these dress shoes without them filling up with a billion granules of the sticky sand. Propping my ass against one of the brick pillars, I slip my shoes off, stuffing my black dress socks into them, and roll up the bottom of my pants. Finally, I'm heading in her direction.

"Hey," I say as I approach, careful not to scare her.

"Hi." She turns around, a small smile on her lips. "I'm sorry I wasn't up at the entrance," she quickly adds, glancing at her watch.

"I'm early," I add. "The bar crowd had thinned out, so she sent me off."

Adeline nods, turning her attention back to the water. "It's so beautiful," she says almost absently.

"It is."

We slowly start to walk, the warm, wet sand squishing between my toes with each step I take. "I see the ocean every day, but never enjoy it." There's great sadness in her words, and my heart can't help but feel for her.

"No?" I ask casually, gently swinging my shoes as we stroll.

"No. We have a spectacular view of the harbor from our offices." She gives a humorless laugh. "Well, not mine. I barely have a window and share a space with another attorney."

Good thing it's dark outside, because I'm unable to hide the shock from my features. "You're an attorney?"

She nods, and again, there's a deep dejection in that one action. "I am. Graduated top of my class from Yale last spring."

"Wow, that's amazing," I reply, unable to keep my awe out of my comment. I suspected Adeline came from money, but I'll admit, I assumed that's the extent of it. I didn't realize she went to school—and not just any school, but a prestigious one like Yale—to become a lawyer.

She shrugs her thin shoulders that always seem to carry so much weight. "Thank you. I hope to one day be able to utilize my degree for more than just a little research and behind the scenes work."

Something tells me there's more to this story, but I'm not sure we're at a place where she wants to confide in me with such personal information. Yes, I'm a bartender, and many people utilize me as their private therapist, but I'm not sure Adeline is one of those individuals. Plus, when she was referring to work or anytime she was on her phone, there was a heaviness to her I didn't like, and I have a feeling it's best to avoid that particular topic.

For now.

"Wanna go see one of my favorite places?" I ask, changing the subject.

She gives me a skeptical look, but quickly replaces it with bravery. "Yes."

Stopping, I turn and face her. I drop my shoes in the sand and place gentle hands on her upper arms. "You don't have to worry about me, Addi. You're safe with me."

"I know," she quickly replies. "I—I wouldn't have invited you to join me tonight if I didn't feel safe, Decker."

Nodding, I release my hold on her, even though I'd much rather have my hands on her, and grab my shoes. We walk side by side, and I realize her sandals are in her left hand, leaving her right free for me to hold. I slip my hand around hers, her slender fingers entwining with mine, and a weird feeling settles in my chest. I feel...alive, yet so peaceful at the same time.

We walk down the beach, away from the resort, and toward the pier. The waves roll at our feet, coating my pants from the knees down in water, but it doesn't bother me at all. If Adeline wants to walk in the surf, then I'll endure any amount of wet clothing to keep that small smile on her beautiful face.

"It's not far now. We're going right up here," I tell her as the landscape around us starts to change a bit. We move from the flat, pristine sandy beaches to a slightly hilly area with large boulders and mossy grass.

"Watch your step. The rocks can come out of nowhere," I tell her, suddenly wishing I had reconsidered my destination. This area isn't necessarily dangerous, but when people start to climb around the rocks, there have been slight injuries.

We carefully make our way to the pier, the waves crashing around the white painted pylons protruding from the water. Adeline stops directly beneath the pier and gazes out. "This is beautiful," she tells me, holding on to my hand a little tighter than before.

"I like to come down here and watch the waves roll in."

"I can see why you like it so much. You could just sit back and get lost in your thoughts so easily," she whispers, as if she's picturing doing just that.

"Very easy to do," I concede, dropping my shoes on a rock and taking hers to do the same. "Where's your purse?" I ask, noticing its absence for the first time.

"I took it up to my room to keep it from getting wet," she states casually, turning her body to face the surf.

"Ahh. That makes sense," I say, wanting to touch her so damn bad, yet needing her to give me a bit of direction here before I do.

She turns her blue gaze my way, a hint of mischief reflecting in them. "Want to know where I hid my room key?"

Her question shocks me and makes my dick hard at the same time. My eyes skim down every delectable curve of her body. She's wearing a sundress that hits just below her knees, her shoulders and arms bare, and I've never wanted to kiss a woman more than I want to kiss her.

A smirk spreads across my face. "Depends. Are you going to tell me...or show me?"

The sweetest bubble of laughter erupts from her mouth. "Definitely show you," she teases, that glint of something naughty reflecting in the blue pools of her eyes.

I watch as she reaches into the cleavage between her breasts and pulls the keycard out. "I have to admit, it's a little more uncomfortable than I was anticipating," she says, looking down at the plastic card.

"Yeah? I can see that."

"Well, that and the fact a million other hands have touched this little card. I actually used a disinfectant wipe before I tucked it away," she informs me, sliding the card back where she got it on the side of her left breast. "I don't know how girls hide money and other items in their bras. It's incredibly unsanitary."

Shaking my head, I give in to the lighthearted laughter threatening to spill from my lips. "I didn't think about that, but you're right. Kinda gross, now that I think about it."

"Right?"

"Come on, rebel Addi. Let's walk out onto the pier," I offer, taking her hand and guiding her around to the steps. There's a slight breeze as we make our way across the water, but the view is worth it. At least, it is to me. I hope Adeline feels the same.

When we reach the end, she stops at the railing and gazes out at the vast sea of dark water in front of us. I position myself directly behind her, releasing her hand just so I can hold her in another way. With my hands on her hips, I rest my chin against her bare shoulder, her perfume tickling my nose and making my cock hard. All I want to do is press it into the cleft of her ass, but we're not quite there yet. If I've read her correctly, she wants something from me, but until she voices that, I'll keep myself in check.

"There's something different about being on the ocean here," she whispers, leaning her head back against my shoulder and gazing up at the starlit sky.

"That's because you're on vacation," I tell her, unable to stop myself from turning into her scent and running my nose along the side of her neck.

"Hmm," she mumbles, that single sound causing my balls to tighten. "Probably, but it's just…different here. Good different."

I nod slightly, the movement bringing my lips in contact with that soft, fragrant skin. "I agree. I grew up in Virginia, and there's definitely something magical to the ocean down in Florida."

Adeline leans to the side just a touch, opening up the long column of her neck even more. I want to trace every square inch of it with my lips. "I've been to Virginia a few times. Their coast is beautiful too."

"It is."

"What brought you to Florida?" she whispers, shifting her hips just a bit and rocking back against my tight body. She doesn't say anything about my hard cock, but there's no way she could have missed it.

Trying to decide how much I want to share of my life and my past, I opt for the simplest truth I have. "Freedom."

She cocks her head so she's looking up at me. For several long moments, she doesn't say a word, and when she does finally speak, her words are, again, dripping with sadness. "I envy you."

"Don't," I tell her, recalling the angry words thrown before I stormed out the door and never returned. "Everyone's road is paved differently."

She returns her gaze to the ocean in front of her. "I couldn't agree with you more." Then she looks up at me, her soulful eyes locking on mine and burning me with the truth and fear I see reflecting in them.

"Sometimes the ones who are supposed to love you the most are the ones who do the most damage."

Nodding, I'm unable to keep my mouth away from hers any longer. I bend down, letting my lips graze across hers softly. "You have the prettiest mouth I've ever seen."

Warm breath tickles my face as she huffs a giggle. "I have to admit, that's the first time someone has complimented my mouth before."

"Really? I find that hard to believe. Your lips are full and the perfect shade of pink," I insist, gently moving my slightly rougher ones against hers. "I've been thinking about kissing you since the moment I saw you."

"Really?"

"Yes," I confess, my hands carefully moving to her front and positioning themselves low on her stomach. "All night when you were at the rehearsal dinner."

"Interesting, because all through this evening, I've found myself thinking about you kissing me as well."

"Yeah?" I ask, barely moving against her lips. "What did you think about?"

Adeline slowly turns, keeping her mouth poised near my lips as her arms wrap around my shoulders. She presses her chest to mine, her lower stomach brushing against my erection. "I wondered what it would be like to invite you to my room."

"What would we do if I accepted your invitation?" I ask, my heart hammering a heavy beat in my chest as anticipation floods my veins.

"You would make me forget," she whispers, her words both in sorrow and a plea.

"What do you want to forget, Addi?"

"Everything. Everything but you and me."

"Just for one night?"

She shrugs, her manicured nails dancing up my neck and sliding into my hair. "Maybe two. Three, tops."

"You're not leaving with the others?" I ask, needing confirmation, considering the rest of the wedding party seems to be heading out.

She shakes her head, those lush lips gliding against mine with her movement. "No. I've decided to add a week to my stay and enjoy a little relaxation."

The corners of my mouth curl upward and my hands flex against her lower back. "What I have in mind for you doesn't scream relaxation, Addi."

She smiles a cat that ate the canary grin as she goes up on her tiptoes and nips at my bottom lip. "I like the idea of screaming."

My cock jumps in my trousers, and it takes every ounce of self-control I possess to not just throw her over my shoulder and carry her to the nearest private room. "What exactly do you want, Addi? Tell me."

She presses herself against me even more and meets my gaze. "Just you. For a night or two. I want to not think about the stuff waiting for me at home. I want to enjoy myself at this stunning resort with a man I'm incredibly attracted to, and maybe even have an orgasm or two along the way."

I'm unable to control my wide, knowing smile. "An orgasm or two?" I ask, leaning in and hovering my mouth over her ear. "Beautiful Addi, an orgasm or two? That'll be just the first hour. If you want me for a few nights, I'm yours, but how about this. As long as you're here, I'm your guy, okay? No strings. Just fun."

She shivers and turns to look me in the eyes, those blue orbs blazing with desire. "No strings. Just fun. For one week." Swallowing, she lifts her chin and asks, "My room okay?"

"Yes." My cock is so hard, I can barely think.

She pulls back and takes my hand with hers. "Let's go."

Chapter FIVE

Adeline

My heart is going to beat out of my chest. I'm going to have a stroke right here on the beach before I get the orgasm or two he's promising. That would be my luck, wouldn't it? Finally taking something for myself and I'll die before I even get a chance to enjoy it. Never mind the fact he's bold enough to guarantee the orgasms I desperately crave. The last man I dated never took off his socks when we had sex, let alone could last long enough to ensure I received release too.

Do you know how many times I had to get myself off in the shower post-sex?

Too many times to count.

Something tells me Decker will ensure I receive my fair share of orgasms. He has this glint in his eyes, this naughty promise that makes me a little weak in the knees and a flood of wetness appear between my legs.

Grabbing our shoes, he takes my hand once more and we hurry back to the resort. The warm breeze kisses my skin, but all I feel is the prickle of anticipation. I've never done anything like this in my life, and the excitement and eagerness is almost too much. It lives between us like a tangible being, thriving off each of us and building with every step we take.

When we reach the cobblestone walkway, he pauses and turns to face me. "I don't have to go up there with you. The control is completely in your hands."

Still holding my sandals, I slide my free hand up his chest and lean in. "I thought guys were always on board for no-strings sex."

The corner of his mouth curls upward. "Oh, I'm on board, but only if you're one-hundred-percent sure. Even if we get up to your room and you change your mind, I won't complain."

Feeling bold because of him, I slip my hand down and tap his erection, making him jump. "You sure you won't complain?"

"There's a difference between needing to go home and jerk off and throwing a fit because you changed your mind."

Clearing my throat, trying to fight that particular image from invading my brain and failing miserably, I add, "Thank you. And for the record, I trust you. I wouldn't be inviting you to my room if I didn't. I've seen late-night *Dateline* shows about single women at resorts."

Decker snorts. "Not saying it won't happen, but Belisa is safe. I've been here about nine months and never seen, nor heard, so much as an issue. There are cameras everywhere, including the hallways and private behind-the-scenes areas like laundry and food service. All employees undergo a background check. The management here is superb, and safety and comfort for those who stay here is top priority."

"Thank you," I reply, feeling even better about my decision to stay here, and also to invite Decker to my room.

He places his lips gently against mine. "Do you still want to go upstairs?"

"Yes," I reply, leaning into him once more, the hard muscles of his chest driving me wild. I haven't even seen them yet, but I can tell he's incredibly fit.

With a grin, he takes my hand once more and escorts me into the hotel. The air-conditioning is cold against my wet skin, the hem of my dress clinging to my legs. I glance over to the front desk, but the man behind it pays us no attention. I was prepared to see that knowing smirk on his face, but he just looked away, his gaze returning to whatever task he was completing instead of following our progress to the bank of elevators.

"Cold?" he asks when we pause in front of the elevator, waiting.

"A little."

Something crosses through his brown eyes that makes my thighs clench. "Give me three minutes and I will warm you up."

The door opens with a ding and we both enter in a rush. The moment the doors close behind us and the floor number is pushed, I'm being pressed against the back wall by a hard body. My leg hitches up, hooking around his thigh. Zings of pleasure course through me as my most intimate place comes in contact with his.

"You're driving me absolutely fucking wild," he mutters against my neck, his lips scraping against my flesh.

A whimper falls from my mouth as my head drops back. "Me too."

The ding sounds louder than usual, causing me to jump. Decker chuckles under his breath and pulls back a bit. He reaches down and picks up my sandals. I didn't even realize I had dropped them. My legs are a bit wobbly, but I somehow manage to walk from the elevator to my new room. I've only been in here twice—once after I checked in and moved my belongings and then when I dropped off my clutch before heading to the beach.

It takes me a second to pull my keycard from my bra and slip it inside the door. The moment the light turns green, Decker turns the handle and steps back to allow me to enter. Once in the room, I drop my keycard on the desk and turn to face the man behind me. He's taking in the space, his eyes pausing for several seconds at the sliding glass door.

When I went to see about availability for the next week, I was happy to hear they had a vacant room with an ocean view and balcony. If I was going to ignore my obligations and my father, at least I was doing it with a fantastic view and the ocean saltiness hanging in the air.

"Your room is nice," he says, walking over to the door and sliding it open. "Do you mind?"

I shake my head. "Not at all. Would you like a drink?" I ask, moving to the mini fridge to see what they offer. "There's water, juice, and little bottles of vodka and tequila."

He slowly moves toward me. No, moves isn't accurate. He stalks toward me, like a lion would his prey, and something tells me I'm about to be eaten alive. "I'm okay right now," he says softly, reaching down and helping me stand. "Would you like something to drink?"

I shake my head, holding his gaze with mine.

A smile spreads across his lips as he reaches for my hip and draws me closer. His mouth moves in, skimming across the column of my neck and dragging across my collarbone. "Is this okay?"

A shiver sweeps through my limbs at the heat and husk in his voice. "Yes," I reply, grabbing on to his forearms and holding on tight.

"Can we take off this dress?"

Fighting against the desire to close my eyes and just feel, I turn my head and find his gaze. "You don't have to ask permission every step of the way, Decker. I want this. I want you. I won't break."

Something fires to life in his eyes as they slowly turn from a deep brown to almost black. He inhales a shuddered breath and lets it out slowly. "I just don't want to move faster than you're prepared to move."

Reaching for the zipper running along the side of my dress, I lower it until the dress hangs open from my armpit to my waist. "Sometimes fast is the only speed to travel."

"If it's too fast though, tell me."

Slipping the spaghetti straps off each shoulder, I shimmy until the dress pools at my feet, and I'm left standing in a strapless bra and matching pair of panties. "I will. Now, Decker?"

"Hmm?" he asks, his eyes drinking in my tall, slender body.

"Take off your clothes."

My words seem to spring him into action as a devilish grin spreads across his gorgeous face. "Yes, ma'am." Reaching for his necktie, he tugs at the knot positioned at the base of his throat and adds, "Leave everything else in place. I'm going to strip you naked and devour your body."

Again, I shiver in anticipation, and watch with bated breath as he slips off his tie and tosses it onto the floor. He then moves to the small buttons on his white button-down, the shirt hanging open with each one released. Finally, when the shirt is unbuttoned, he removes the black belt around his waist and unclasps the single black button. He quickly follows that up with lowering the zipper, but doesn't make a move to take his pants or shirt the rest of the way off.

"Don't look at me like that," he demands.

"I was kind of hoping you'd lose the pants too," I quip, reaching out and running my finger down the thin strip of dark hair running from his belly button to where his pants hang open.

"If I take them off, I'll fuck you."

My eyebrows draw heavenward. "Isn't that the goal here?"

He takes a step back so I'm no longer touching him, and smiles. "Oh, it most definitely is, but not yet. First, I'm going to eat your pussy until you come."

I swallow over the sudden dryness in my throat. "Yes, please."

He chuckles, slipping the dress shirt off and tossing it on the table. "Lie back." As I turn toward the bed, he adds, "Not the bed, Addi. I want you on that chair."

My eyes move to the chaise chair in the corner of the room near the balcony. It looks incredibly comfortable, and I'll admit, lying on it with the ocean crashing on the beach below me sounds amazing, but...

Decker turns, walking away, and suddenly I wonder if I took too long to do as he instructed. However, as clean as I'm sure this resort is, my mind just won't stop going there now that the idea seed has been planted.

He returns from the bathroom a second later holding a towel. Without even looking at the questions swimming in my eyes, he lays it down on the chaise so my ass wouldn't be directly on the seat. "I could see the unease in your eyes," he says, making my entire body relax a bit and my heart skip a beat.

I've never had someone take my personal issues into account as much as he does. I'm not a germaphobe, but there are just certain things that tend to make my icky-scale tilt a little more than others. I know hotels are usually on the cleaner side, especially an upper scale resort like this, but still. I see the chair and I wonder how many naked rear ends have sat in it since it was last cleaned.

"Is this okay?"

Nodding, I reach out and squeeze his arm, telling him thank you without saying the words.

"Good. Now get your gorgeous body on the chair, Addi. My mouth is dying to taste you."

I practically jump onto the chair in the least graceful way possible, resulting in a chuckle from Decker. I lean against the back of the chair, my legs stretched out in front of me. "Like this?"

"Perfect. Now, let your thighs fall open."

Bringing my feet together, I do as instructed, letting my thighs open widely against the armrests. Not really sure what to do with my hands, I let one relax at my side, while the other goes over my head.

"I almost don't want to take that pink satin off your body, but at the same time, I'm afraid if I don't, I might explode," he quips, reaching for my feet and spreading them apart. Then, he climbs between them, resting his chest on the chair and kisses my inner thigh.

A gasp slips from my lips as I watch his tongue dance along my skin, slowly making its way to the apex of my legs. My blood is humming through my veins, my body tight with desire and eagerness.

"Pull that bra down, Addi. I want to see those beautiful tits while I'm eating your pussy."

I practically convulse at the rawness in his words. I've never been with a man who was so vocal in bed the way Decker is, and I'm starting to think I've been left severely lacking in the sexual partners category over the years.

Slipping the strapless bra down, I expose my breasts to the man between my legs. I don't have much upstairs. With my tall, slender frame, God didn't grace me with big, perky breasts the way he did so many other women. Instead, I have a small B-cup and have always been so envious of those around me with the perfect hourglass shape.

"My God, you're stunning," he insists, licking his lips as he stares at my chest.

"They're small," I blurt out, causing my cheeks to blush by my direct statement.

"No, they're perfect. As soon as I eat your pussy and make you come, I'll show you just how much I love them," he replies, adding a cocky wink before lowering his mouth to my panties once more. "Are these expensive?"

"What?"

"These," he says, running his finger across the pink satin between my legs.

I open my mouth, but nothing comes out. Are they expensive? Yes. But curiosity gets the best of me, and I have to know why he's asking. "Not terribly so," I reply.

I'm rewarded with a wolfish grin. "Perfect."

Decker lowers his mouth to the material and licks straight up the seam of my body. Fire shoots throughout me as he grabs the side and pulls it over, exposing my wet core. Then, finally, he makes contact with my skin. He drags his tongue from the bottom of my sex across my clit, sending shock waves of pleasure screaming through my veins.

"Mmm," he moans against my flesh, his mouth vibrating in the best way possible. "So fucking good."

My nipples pebble hard as I close my eyes, the sensations already intense. He delves his tongue deep inside me, drawing a low moan of pleasure from my lungs. The noise I make seems to spur him on, as he continues to slide his tongue inside my body. His hands rest on my thighs, gently pressing them open as far as possible. Shifting his position, he's able to still hold my legs with his thumbs and skim his middle fingers across my swollen clit. The action causes me to jolt once more, the release already starting to build.

Again, he shifts, and suddenly, his finger is poised at my entrance and slowly pressing inside. Instantly, I feel the stretch of his invasion, at the fullness it possesses. He pushes it fully inside, curling his finger upward. Before I can even appreciate the feeling of him inside me, he's pulling it out and doing it again. Only this time, there's a greater stretch as he uses two fingers.

Then, he places his open mouth over my clit and sucks. I cry out, the release that's been building erupting with a force I've never felt in my entire life. My eyes squeeze shut as wave after wave of euphoric bliss takes over me. I can feel myself clamp around his fingers, but that doesn't stop him from moving those fingers and drawing out every ounce of pleasure from my body.

"Uncle," I whisper when I realize he's not stopping.

His chuckle sends vibrations through my sensitive lady bits. "You're calling it already? Addi, I was just getting started," he insists with a big grin on his face. There's wetness on his chin. I don't know what I expect, but it isn't for him to lick his lips as if he were getting every drop.

"What else did you have in mind?" I ask, playing coy.

"I could tell you," he starts, standing up and hooking his hands in the sides of his dress slacks. "But I think I'd rather show you."

And then he pushes the pants down.

My mouth waters as I stare at his erection. It's evident he wasn't wearing underwear, and I have no idea why that excites me as much as it does. Add in the fact he's long, hard, and very ready, and I'm quite certain I'm in for a night I won't ever forget.

Suddenly, I'm not as spent as I was only a handful of seconds ago. My core is flooding with wetness once more, my nipples beading in anticipation. I'm sure my heart is trying to leap from my chest, but even that won't dull this incredible need I have for this man. Something tells me I'm about to embark on the ride of my life.

I can't wait.

"All right, Decker. Show me."

Chapter SIX

Decker

Show me.

Two simple words, yet together, holding more power than I've ever experienced.

Adeline is splayed out before me, her fancy satin panties pulled off to the side and disfigured, her nipples hard and on full display, calling to my mouth.

I step out of my pants and kick them to the side before reaching for my cock and giving it a hard squeeze. Precum seeps from the tip and my balls draw up. I have a feeling this is going to be fast. Seeing her body before me, hearing her words, is like adding gasoline to an already blazing inferno.

"On the bed, beautiful," I instruct, my voice husky with desire even to my own ears.

Gracefully, she rises from the chaise chair and moves to the bed. I get there first, pulling the white comforter down. Adeline climbs onto the bed, her hair a mess of blond tendrils all over the pillows. I reach for the wallet tucked inside my back pants pocket and pull out a condom, my eyes continually returning to where she lies.

So soft.

So sweet.

So fucking mine.

For tonight.

I toss the condom onto the bed beside her and climb on, covering her body with my own. I drag my lips from her belly button to her tits, sucking each nipple into my hot mouth. I was right. She's so respon-sive, her nipples hard and perfect for my mouth. When she starts to wiggle beneath me, I release my hold on her with a pop and kneel beside her. First, I slip the panties down her long legs before removing the bra. She sits up but doesn't say a word, before lying back down the moment she's completely naked.

Grabbing the protection, I quickly rip it open and sheathe my cock. Her eyes follow my every move, her pink tongue slipping out to lick her lips. Giving myself one more squeeze, I ask, "You want your mouth on my cock, Addi?"

She nods.

"Soon. First, I'm going to fuck an orgasm out of you. Then, I want to see those lips wrapped around my cock."

Adeline whimpers, her eyes glazed over with lust as I move into position. The head of my cock lines up with her pussy, my body begging to thrust inside her. I hold back though, sliding my dick against her clit, teasing her entrance before pressing just the tip inside her warmth. I'm about to ask her if she's sure, but she takes the ques-tion right out of my head by grabbing my ass with both hands and pulling me forward. There's no time to catch myself. I'm thrust inside her, balls deep in one stroke. It feels fucking earth-shattering, exactly what you think heaven would feel like, but it's short-lived as she completely tenses at the invasion.

"Shit, Addi," I mutter, trying to hold myself up and keep from moving. "Relax."

I bend down and take her mouth with mine, coaxing open her lips and letting my tongue do the talking. After a few seconds, I feel her internal muscles start to release their hold on my dick, allowing me to move a little more freely again.

"That's it, Addi," I whisper, slowly pulling out and gently sliding back in. "You feel fucking amazing," I add, gently starting to move my hips. "So damn tight and perfect."

She groans, arching her back as I bottom out. "So good," she mumbles.

Reaching down, I hitch one leg up on my hip, spreading her wider and giving me a little more room to work. I lower my mouth to her tits once more, loving the way they bounce against my lips with each thrust of my hips.

Her hands move to my back, her nails digging into my flesh. I can feel my balls already tighten, the need to find release looming nearby. She's too fucking tight and wet to ignore much longer. My body is starting to move on its own. My hips thrust with a little more force. The sweet noises she makes only encourage me on, and all too soon, I'm unable to slow or stop what's coming.

She's close. I can tell, but she's not there, and I need her to be. Reaching between us, I apply a little pressure to her clit and roll it between my fingers as I thrust into her. Adeline cries out again. "Oh, God," she mutters moments before she explodes, her pussy squeezing the life out of my cock and triggering my release instantly.

That familiar tingle races up my spine. "Fuck," I mumble, my eyes trying to cross as the pleasure races through my veins. I force myself to watch her, to memorize the way she moves beneath me, the way she feels wrapped around my cock, and the way she looks as her orgasm consumes her. If I never have the chance to be in this woman again, at least I'll have the memories of this one night burned into my brain like a vibrant tattoo. Something I'll be able to gaze upon when I close my eyes on the nights I'm alone in the shower.

She calls my name as she rides the final waves of her release, her nails biting my flesh and marking me. I could not care less though. I'll wear those scratches like a badge of fucking honor, proudly showing them off whenever I can.

When my arms are no longer able to hold me up, I fall forward, caging her against the mattress. My mouth is there, claiming hers with a gentle, yet searing kiss. This is something else that makes Adeline different. My mouth can't seem to stop touching her.

Finally, I drop to my side, slipping an arm beneath her neck as I rest on the pillow. I know I need to get up. I have a condom to contend with, but there's also the fact I'm not staying here. This was sex. Great sex. Out of this world, memorable in every way sex, and to be honest, I'm not sure I've had my fill of her yet.

My cock threatening to thicken once more tells me I'm not.

But still sex, and I'm not expecting to stay.

"Wow," she whispers, her backside pressing against my stomach as she curls onto her side.

"Mmm." My lips trail kisses down her neck and shoulder.

With my hand on her hip, I nuzzle her, inhaling her sweet scent. "I should go take care of the condom, but I have to admit, I'm having a hard time getting up right now."

She wiggles her ass against my cock, and the bastard is suddenly hard once more. "Seems to me you're not having any trouble getting up."

I can't help but chuckle, as I place a chaste, hard kiss on her shoulder. "I'll be right back."

Then, I force my legs to move and climb from the bed. I head for the bathroom and close the door, grateful to have a few minutes alone to get myself together. Yes, I enjoyed the sex, but it felt a little too good holding her afterward. After taking care of the condom, I use the restroom and wash up a little. My cock is still half-hard. It's as if he knows she's outside the bathroom.

Knowing the awkward conversation is upon us, I pull open the door, only to find a very naked Adeline standing there. She's moving, plastering herself against me before I can even comprehend what's happening. Reaching down, my hands cup the globes of her perfect ass, my cock wedged and standing at full attention between us.

"I thought, maybe, you could use a shower."

Every reason why I should leave just evaporates from my brain. "I could use a shower," I reason, walking backward into the room. My mouth takes hers, the kiss hot and ravenous.

Her hands are everywhere. Running down my chest, reaching between us to stroke my dick. I suck in a shuddered breath before lifting her onto the counter between the sinks. Her legs wrap around my waist, drawing me in with her siren's song.

"I was lying out there, thinking," she starts, stroking my cock with her delicate fingers.

"Yeah? What were you thinking about?"

"About your…cock." A light blush tinges her cheeks pink, and I can't help but smile. Since the moment I laid eyes on Adeline, I knew using a vulgar vocabulary wasn't her norm, so to hear her say the word cock excites me even more.

"What about it? What do you want to do with my cock?" I ask, closing my eyes momentarily while she continues to move her hand.

"I think...Well, I'd like to allow you to...you know," she mumbles and fumbles.

"Don't get shy on me now, Addi. I want to hear you say the words. What do you want to do with my cock?" I repeat, blood swooshing through my veins as I anxiously await.

She takes a deep breath and meets my gaze. "I want you to...fuck me...with your amazing cock."

I groan. "My pleasure, beautiful. Stay right here," I demand, placing a chaste kiss on her lips before I practically run from the bathroom to grab my wallet. Fortunately, there's one condom left inside.

When I return, her legs are pressed together, that sexy blush covering her chest and tits. "Spread your legs, Addi."

She does immediately, while I rip open the condom and cover myself.

Stepping between her legs, my dick nudges her opening, and I couldn't be more grateful for how perfect we seem to fit. I've never dated a woman as tall as her, only a couple of inches shorter than my six-foot frame, but I don't care. I don't need to tower over a woman to make myself feel big. Watching her eyes glaze over as I make her come does that tenfold.

Placing my hands on the counter at her hips, I press inside. She whimpers at the invasion, hitching both legs over my hips as much as she can. I try to go slow, to give her time to adjust to my size, but Adeline has other plans. She grabs my ass once more, rocking her hips as much as she can while pulling me toward her.

"So good," she whispers, trailing her lips across my collarbone.

"Fuck yes," I reply, already feeling my own body starting to coil tight.

I continue to move slowly, not wanting to hurt her, but this woman has other plans. She pushes me back gently, dislodging my cock, and hops down. "There's something I've always wanted to do."

She turns around and bends over the counter, her beautiful ass pushed out toward me. "Ahh, fuck," I mutter, my cock jerking eagerly as I look up to meet her gaze in the mirror. "You want me to fuck you from behind?"

Adeline shivers in response.

Stepping forward, I line myself up and gently press inside. We both moan together as I grip her hips in my hands, needing something to hold on to. Adeline arches her back, the image before me something straight out of my fantasies. She meets my gaze in the mirror, her eyes pleading with me to move.

So I do.

My fingers dig into her flesh as I pull back and rocket forward. She's already squeezing around me, which only seems to spur me further. I piston my hips, encouraged with each grunt and moan from her lips. I don't think I've ever seen something as beautiful as what I'm watching play out in the mirror.

Adeline reaches between her legs. My eyes devour the sight of her sliding her fingers against her clit. My hands move to her shoulders, gently lifting her so I get a better view. Her eyes flutter closed as I pound into her from behind. My balls are tight and the tingle shoots up my spine.

"Decker," she mutters, and that's all it takes for me to explode for a second time tonight. Adeline follows, gripping my dick like a vise as she comes along with me.

I force my eyes to remain locked on her, to watch as a look of pure bliss transforms her face. When my body is too spent to move anymore, I lean forward, my mouth dragging against her bare skin. "It's official. You're trying to kill me."

She chuckles, making her internal muscles vibrate against me. "No way. I enjoy this too much to kill you off. I'm sort of hoping for another round, possibly after a little nap," she says, triggering a yawn.

"Hmm, another round, huh? I need to make a trip to the store first."

She slowly starts to stand up, so I take a step back, dislodging my very sated cock from her once more. "You know, I believe there's a small place down by the lobby. I'm sure they sell them," she informs, turning around and leaning against the counter. Her fingers move to touch my chest, softly trailing down my skin.

"Yes, I'm sure they do, but I think I'd rather buy condoms from a place where I *don't* work."

The sweetest giggle seeps from her lips. "Oh. Yes, that's probably best," she says through another yawn.

"You should go to bed," I tell her, swiping the hair off her forehead.

She smiles at the touch. "Only if you come too."

"I have. Twice," I quip, even though I know that's not what she meant.

She smacks my shoulder with a laugh. "You know what I meant. I was thinking…" she starts, nibbling on her bottom lip.

I reach down and slide the condom off, tossing it into the trash can. "About what?" I ask, turning my full attention back to her.

Her cheeks turn pink, and I can tell she's building the courage to say what's on her mind. Waiting her out, she finally opens her mouth and asks, "I was thinking, perhaps you'd like to stay the night?" Before I can say a word, she continues. "I know whatever this is is just…fun and temporary, but I'm here for the next week, and I have to be honest, I've never had a man…do the things you do."

My eyebrows draw together. "The things I do?"

She nods quickly. "Yes. Orgasms. Lots of them."

A wolfish smile spreads across my lips. "So, you're proposing I give you more orgasms while you're here?"

She cringes a little. "My word, that sounds scandalous and crude when you say it like that."

I wrap my hand around her waist and draw her close. "It's not. It's blunt and sexy as hell. We're both single, attracted to each other, and clearly, have sexual chemistry in spades."

She runs her hands up my chest. "We do."

"Then, I would be honored to give you plenty of orgasms while you're here."

Adeline smiles at me. "Great. I'd love to receive plenty more."

A bark of laughter erupts from my lungs as I shake my head at her comment. "You're trouble, you know that?"

"Actually, I'm not. I've never been trouble a day in my life. I'm quite the opposite, I assure you."

"Well, we can chalk this up to the new you. While you're here, you're trouble, but do you know what?" When she looks at me with question in her blue eyes, I add, "I really like your kinda trouble."

She doesn't reply, just yawns.

"Come on, beautiful. Let's get you to bed."

A devilish smirk teases her lips. "Are you sure we shouldn't shower first?"

"Later. I need you well rested if I'm going to have my wicked way with you again," I insist, taking her hand and escorting her back to bed.

"Yes, please," she whispers, climbing into the bed and reaching for the rumpled white sheet. The moment her head hits the pillow, it comes up again. "You're staying, right?"

"If you want me to," I reply, my heart doing this weird rapid beat in my chest.

She rests her head on the pillow once more and closes her eyes. "I do. Wake me up when it's time to shower. I'd really like to take you in my mouth. You know, see what the fuss is all about?"

My cock kicks against my leg. I have questions to ask in reference to her statement, but now isn't the time. Her mouth is already falling open as she begins to drift off to sleep.

I head for the door and flip the deadbolt. Then, I walk over to the sliding door, which is still open, and step onto the balcony, not caring I'm as naked as the day I was born. I'm met with the sound of the ocean and gulls squawking on the beach. I'm almost afraid to look around, recalling exactly how loud we were when I was fucking her—both times—but am relieved to not find an audience nearby. In fact, no one seems to be awake.

I step back inside and pull the door closed, securing the lock. A part of me says to grab my clothes and hit the road, but then I spot Adeline lying in bed, her bare back and the top of her ass angled my way, and I know there's no way I'm leaving. Not with this beautiful woman offering me a week of no-strings sex if I stay.

My feet move in her direction, and I flip off the small wall lamp beside the bed. It was on when we arrived in her room, and even though she's able to sleep with it on now, I don't want her to wake before necessary because of a damn light.

The room is dark, only the moonlight filtering through the glass door creating enough glow to see. I slip into bed behind her, my arms automatically pull her close. She sighs and nestles into my pillow, her body pressed tightly against mine. I've never been a snuggler. I'm a hot bastard, always preferring to sleep naked, with a sheet and a fan, but having Adeline here isn't so bad.

In fact, it's pretty fucking comfortable.

Her smooth, soft skin against mine.

That's the last thing I remember as I close my eyes and let sleep consume me.

Chapter SEVEN

Adeline

I slowly wake to the sound of ocean waves and the scent of coffee mixed with the salty sea hanging in the air. I stretch my legs and arms out, feeling a tightness in my muscles in multiple places, but it's the soreness between my legs that catches my attention. A slow smile spreads across my face as I remember exactly how I received the stiffness that seems to plague me.

Realizing the bed is empty, I move to my elbows to have a look around. Decker is on the balcony, wearing his trousers and sipping what I assume is a cup of coffee. From this angle, I'm able to enjoy an unobstructed view of the man I spent the night with. He's incredibly fit, but isn't just ripped with muscles, and he has tattoos. I noticed the ones on his arms when I first saw him, but now, under the warm, bright sun, I'm able to see the words across his left shoulder blade.

Be free it says in a scratchy, shaky font.

As if sensing my eyes on him, he turns and looks over his shoulder. A warm smile spreads across his lips. Lips that did incredible things to me in the wee hours of the morning. "Morning," he says, heading into the suite.

"Good morning," I reply, holding the sheet up to my chest as I sit up. "Have you been up a while?"

"No, about thirty minutes or so," he replies, sitting on the bed beside me. "How'd you sleep?"

"Like the dead," I mutter, averting my gaze. My eyes just want to drink in his hard chest and study the black ink on his arms.

"Me too." Clearing his throat, he starts, "So, listen, I was thinking—"

"About taking a shower?" I quip, my nipples hardening at the thought.

Decker chuckles and reaches for my hand, pulling it away from my chest. The action allows the sheet to fall to my waist. "Well, yes, that too, but I was also thinking about breakfast," he says, his eyes trained intently on my breasts.

"We could order room service," I offer, not completely opposed to living the next week in this room, naked, with this man.

He reaches out and rubs the pad of his thumb over my hard nipple. Waves of pleasure instantly crash through me. "We could, but I have a better idea. Why don't we go out for breakfast? I'd love to show you around a little bit. You've never been here, right?" he asks, palming my breast in his warm hand.

"N-no," I whisper.

"Hmm," he replies, setting his paper coffee cup down on the night-stand. He moves quickly, getting up on his knees and moving into position. He's so close, the only course of action for me is to lie back, which earns a smile in response. "How about we go to my favorite diner for breakfast, and then we'll go explore?"

I can barely think. His hand is on my stomach, wide and warm, and slowly starts to move downward. My legs spread instantly, which earns me another smile. "I like the idea of…exploring."

"Great. Now, let me eat your pussy until you come, and then we'll go shower for the day. I need to stop by my place and change into something not so wrinkly and dressy though. That okay?" he asks, removing the sheet completely and wedging himself between my thighs.

"Frankly, you could tell me we're going to bomb a small country right now, and I'd happily agree to it." I whimper at the first swipe of his tongue against my swollen flesh.

Decker chuckles. "For the record, I'd never, *ever* do something like that, but good to know you'd do my bidding," he teases before lowering his mouth once again.

I bark out a sharp laugh. "Yes, I'm pretty sure I'd do anything you ask if it means you do *that* more."

He looks up and holds my gaze. "Well, no bombing necessary today, Addi. Just lie back and let me enjoy my pre-shower appetizer."

And I do.

Twice.

"Oh my goodness, this place is so cute," I announce cheerfully the moment his car is parked in the small, gravel driveway.

"The owner lives in the bigger house in front. She became a widow about three years ago and decided to rent out her guesthouse for extra income. She posted an ad online for the small house and was willing to accept my application, despite not being from the area. Her name is Marian, and I'm certain she'll be out to say hello before we reach the door," he replies with a smile.

He's not wrong. As if on cue, an older woman with short gray hair and twinkling brown eyes appears on the sidewalk beside me. "Come on. She's always watching for me, which means she probably saw you the moment I pulled into the driveway."

Releasing my seat belt, I slowly climb from the car and give the old woman a grin. "You must be Marian."

Her eyes brighten with delight. "I am, dear. And you are?"

"I'm Adeline Montgomery," I state, reaching out my hand for her. "Pleasure to meet you."

The woman gently squeezes my hand before turning her attention to Decker. "Hmm, if I recall correctly, you were wearing that yesterday afternoon when you went to work."

Decker laughs, shaking his head, while I feel myself blush, and it has nothing to do with the Florida heat. "Mari, Mari, Mari, what have I told you about snooping?" he asks, his voice laced with humor.

The old woman waves him off. "It's not snooping when you're working in the yard between our houses. Besides, you know I live vicariously through you these days." She turns back to me. "The only time I ever get out is when I have a doctor's appointment."

"When's the next one? I'll make sure I'm off to take you," Decker says, surprising me.

"Not until next month. I'll put a note on your door with the date," Marian says.

Decker nods, reaching for my hand. "Now, if you'll excuse me, I need to go change my clothes." Marian snickers. "Behave, you," he adds, placing a kiss on her aged cheek as he leads me to the front door of the small house he rents.

"I make no promises. Lovely meeting you, dear!" Marian hollers, waving as we go.

"You as well," I reply, unable to stop smiling.

He slides the key into the lock and turns the knob. Cool air-conditioning hits me in the face as we step inside the small house. "Make yourself at home. I'm going to change real quick, and then we can go."

Nodding, my eyes are already scanning the room as he disappears through one of the few doorways. The living room and kitchen are open to each other with a small bar between them. The living room has a brown leather couch, matching chair, and a few mismatched end tables. There's a decent sized television on the far wall, with a small entertainment unit below it. There, I find a handful of movies, a few books, and two framed photographs. One is of a young Decker fishing with an older man, and the other is of the same two men at what I assume is Decker's high school graduation. They're both smiling, arms thrown over each other's shoulders as they hold a diploma between them.

"That's my grandfather. I called him Papa Harry."

I startle, not realizing Decker had reentered the room. "Past tense," I whisper to myself, not meaning to truly speak it aloud.

"Yes. He passed away a few years back," he informs me.

"I'm sorry."

"Thanks. I was closest to him," he adds, looking back at the framed photograph. "Him and Nana Maureen."

"It must be hard losing someone you love like that," I say almost absently.

"You've never lost someone you loved before?" he inquires, leaning against the wall.

Shrugging, I tell him, "I was never close to my family. I have uncles, aunts, and cousins, but the only occasion we saw them was a special event somewhere."

"That's kinda sad," he replies.

"It is," I confirm. "That's why I gravitated toward Audrey when we met. She had this amazing family. They were messy and loud, but they always did normal family things together like dinners. Her parents were in the bleachers at every single sporting event and school function."

"And yours weren't," Decker derives sadly.

"No. Not once. They even missed my college graduation. My father had an important case to prepare for and couldn't be bothered to take the weekend off."

"Shit," he mutters. "And your mother?"

I shrug, fumbling with the sash around the waist of my sundress. "At a spa, I think?"

"Jesus."

Straightening my spine, I state, "My friendship with Audrey has always been important to me. She is the only friend I truly trust, even if we don't get to see each other as much as we'd like. Believe it or not, we're quite the opposite in nearly every way."

Decker smiles. "Yeah, I could see that Friday night at the rehearsal dinner."

I lift my shoulders casually. "It works for us."

"I'm glad. Everyone needs a good friend."

Holding his gaze, I find myself asking, "Do you have a good friend? Someone you can rely on to be in your corner?"

He seems to consider my question for a moment before answering. "I had my grandfather prior to his death. We were incredibly close. Otherwise, I have an old buddy back in Virginia I keep in contact with regularly. He's an investment banker there. Married his high school sweetheart and has three kids. Pretty good dude, even if I don't get to hang out with him like I used to."

I nod, understanding completely. It's not that you don't want to communicate, but life can make it hard. Between work, kids, social obligations, whatever you have, there's never enough hours in the day. Monthly drinks get pushed back and back, and the next thing you know it's been six months or a year since you've gotten to hang out. It's not intentional or malicious. It's life and it flies by. Perhaps it's just an excuse, but when life is pulled in a thousand directions, I can understand how the things you enjoy, those you love, can be slowly pushed to the back burner.

I make a mental note to check on Audrey again soon, especially after the crappy weekend she's had.

The heaviness hangs in the air before he finally clears his throat. "Ready for breakfast?"

Relief washes over me. Not because I'm not comfortable talking to Decker. I am. Surprisingly so, actually, for someone I really just met. But we're getting awfully close to crossing over a more personal, private line. Our time together isn't supposed to be about that. It's supposed to be fun, so while I don't mind sharing a little bit about myself, nor do I not enjoy learning more about the man in front of me, it's best to keep things on the lighter side.

"I'm starving, so yes," I answer, turning away from the framed photos and walking toward the door.

Maybe at another time I would have asked for a tour of his small home, to see the bedroom where he sleeps at night, but right now, I think it's best to head out. He pauses to relock the front door, and while he does, I take a glance around the yard. The backyard is stunning with flower gardens and seating areas. There's even a pond with a waterfall feature, and over by one of the rose bushes is Marian.

"She's out here all day long. It's how she is able to keep tabs on me so much," he says with a chuckle.

"What a beautiful oasis," I say, taking in the breathtaking, large open space.

"Marian was a master gardener, and when she and her husband, Gary, were looking for their next home, she only had one request: a huge backyard to grow her gardens."

"Well, she got that," I reply.

"She did. Gary maintained the house and lawn, but Marian did the rest. They didn't use the guesthouse, so when Gary passed away from an aneurism three years ago, she had her grandson, who's a carpenter, come and give it a face-lift, inside and out.

"I use the private drive off Durham Street, but the main entrance is up front by the house on Louis Drive. When she rented me the house, her only request was that I didn't touch the backyard, which I readily agreed to. I didn't want to be the person who messed up any of her flowers," he says with a chuckle.

"After the first month I was here, I found out she was paying a man to mow the property. He was always late or not showing up at all, so I volunteered to do it for her. She tried to pay me, but I refused. I don't mind helping her with a little mowing. In fact, I rather enjoy it. It's the trimming of the shrubbery and pruning the trees I could live without."

Smiling, I reach over and squeeze his arm. "You're a good man, Decker."

He shrugs off the compliment. "I'm just doing what anyone else would do to help a sweet older lady."

"No, I don't think so. I know many who would rather pay someone to get a task done instead of helping complete it themselves." I try to categorize every man in and out of my life over the last decade and don't come up with a single name of a person who would do what Decker is doing to help his landlord.

"Well, I'm not doing it entirely for free. She does knock twenty dollars off my rent each month," he adds with a smile.

A giggle slips from my mouth. "I can't imagine twenty dollars would go very far in maintaining this yard, and I haven't even seen the front."

He shrugs again, sliding his hands into the pockets of his khaki shorts. "Maybe if it were a twelve-year-old with a summer job."

"Well, that's very admirable of you. I'm sure she appreciates it."

"She does, but I think she appreciates the friendship more. Marian is lonely, but I don't think you could pry her away from this place for anything in the world. This is the home she built with her husband. It's what links her to him, even after he's passed."

My throat gets thick as emotions swell in my chest. My gaze shifts once more to the petite old woman, joyfully working in one of her many flower gardens. She gazes up, a small smile on her lips, as she closes her eyes and lets the warmth of the Florida sun soak into her skin. I can't help but smile too.

"Shall we?" he asks, pulling his right hand from his shorts and extending it toward me.

I place my hand in his. "Sure."

Is it bad I really would enjoy going over to visit with Marian a bit more? Maybe taking a seat under the wooden pergola, amongst the bright yellows, reds, and oranges? I can just picture her serving iced tea or maybe coffee to her guests.

"Maybe we can come back for a visit," he says, as if sensing my hesitancy to leave.

A wide grin spreads across my face. "I'd like that."

He nods once. "She would too. Marian doesn't get many visitors, but I know she enjoys it when she does."

"Perfect. Thank you," I tell him.

"Goodbye, Marian. I'll see you later!" Decker hollers, holding up his left hand in a wave.

She spins around and waves back. "I'll see you when I see you," she teases, a knowing smile on her wrinkled face. "It was lovely to meet you, Adeline. I hope you'll stop by again soon."

"I will," I assure her. Before I can say anything else, the old woman turns her attention back to her flowers and continues to work.

Together, we return to the car, Decker holding open the passenger side door for me. As soon as he slides into the driver's seat, he says, "Barney's has the best crème brûlée French toast."

My stomach growls, my mouth watering at the thought. "Of course. I splurged yesterday and had pancakes for breakfast. Do you know how long it's been since I had pancakes?" I told myself adding the side of fruit made it healthy, but I knew better. Especially since I barely ate any of the fruit accompanying the big, fluffy pancakes.

He gives me a look, backs out of the driveway, and heads toward our destination. "Do I want to know why you don't eat pancakes?"

I shrug, preferring not to answer.

The truth is my mother was the first one to remind me of the consequences of eating high carbs and sugary foods. She was against anything that wasn't salad based, or for a breakfast option, she pushed a poached egg.

"Okay," he says, clearing his throat. "So, we're going to order all the fatty, delicious foods we want and gorge ourselves. You're on vacation, right?"

"Right." I feel the smile take over my lips.

"Right," he repeats, his own smile plastered on his gorgeous face as he reaches over and takes my hand. "Let's go crazy."

"I might regret it later, but I think you're right. I'm on vacation." And it's not like I haven't already conducted myself in less-than-lady-like behavior where he's concerned. "Bring on the French toast."

Chapter EIGHT

Decker

"If I eat another bite, I'll explode," Adeline says, her voice laced with agony as she leans back in the booth.

I can't help but give her a proud smile. She helped consume enough food to feed a large family, and even though I'm quite full myself, I'd gladly devour more if it meant watching her eat. I've watched her two other times, and she was always polite and almost dainty. Today, however, she dove in with gusto, moaning in pleasure with each bite she took.

My cock's been hard for the past twenty minutes.

"Can I get you anything else, Deck?" Yvonne asks, dropping the bill off at our table.

"Nope," I reply, reaching into my pocket and retrieving my wallet.

"Are you kidding me? Did Barney finally do it? Are you full?"

I narrow my eyes at the woman who has served me breakfast at least twice a week since I moved to town nine months ago. "Be nice."

Barney's wife, Yvonne, rolls her eyes and turns her attention to Adeline. "I swear, this boy has a tapeworm."

"Not a boy," I counter, placing my hand on my belly. "I'm a man. A growing man who requires a lot of food."

She tsks, giving me a pointed look as she replies, "He's the reason we had to cancel our Unlimited Pancakes on Tuesdays."

Adeline barks out a laugh, and then covers her mouth with her hand. I point at the older woman. "Stop encouraging her."

Yvonne rolls her eyes once more. "You love me, Decker Paulson."

"Yeah, yeah," I mumble, goodheartedly.

The truth is, I do. I met Yvonne and Barney when I first moved to town and discovered this place. They didn't care I wasn't from here or work a fancy job. They're good people who focus on serving delicious breakfast and lunch menu options and have fun while doing it. It's not a place most tourists visit. It's small and old, but that's okay. I'd rather the place not be overrun with weekenders anyway, and I don't think that's what Barney and Yvonne want either. They are happy just serving the locals seven days a week, and always have a smile on their faces while doing it.

"I'll be back with your change," Yvonne says, grabbing the check and cash I placed on the table.

"Keep it."

She offers me a warm smile. "You're too good to me, Deck. Enjoy the day. Are you going to Marlin's?"

"That's where we're headed next," I tell her, slipping my wallet back into my back pocket as I stand.

"It was so nice to meet you," Adeline says to Yvonne as she stands. "It was delicious. I'm seriously about to burst," she adds with a chuckle.

Yvonne grins from ear to ear. "That's the best compliment we can get. Barney will be pleased to hear."

"Yes, please. I can see why Decker loves it here."

Yvonne just smiles before pulling Adeline into a hug. I can tell Adeline tenses for a moment, clearly not used to being hugged by a stranger, but she doesn't pull away. She just wraps her arms around the older woman's back and gives her a gentle squeeze.

When they release, Yvonne turns my way. "You better bring this one back again."

"I will," I agree, even though I'm not sure I can follow through.

"Good," she states with a proud smile. "Enjoy your day, kids."

I take Adeline's hand and lead her out the door, the familiar bell chiming as we pass through. As we approach my car in the small lot beside the diner, Adeline asks, "What's Marlin's?"

"Marlin's Market. It's a huge farmers market, and they have everything you could possibly imagine," I say, opening up the passenger door.

"Really?" Her eyes dance with excitement. "I've never been to a farmers market before."

"Well, you're in for a treat." Then something else hits me. I glance down and ask, "Those shoes comfortable? You're gonna be doing a lot of walking."

Adeline rolls her eyes and blows out a breath. "Are you kidding me? I'm used to walking sixteen hours a day in Louboutins. A couple of hours at a farmers market in sandals will be no sweat."

My eyes drop down to her legs. The thought of her toned calves on display in sexy black fuck-me heels does a little something below the belt, if you know what I mean. "I think I want to see that." Shutting the door, I adjust my cock as inconspicuously as possible, and head to the driver's seat. "All right, Miss Montgomery. Your day of adventure awaits."

"Look at these!" Adeline bellows, pointing at one of the booths we're approaching and pulling me in that direction.

I think I've been smiling since the moment we got here, because watching the joy and excitement on her face just seems to bring it out of me too. I'm carrying bags of fresh pastries and baked goods, flowers, and handmade trinkets she couldn't pass up, and if I had to guess, in a minute, I'll be adding fresh fruit to our haul.

"How much?" she asks the woman behind the table.

"Four for a dollar," the polite woman informs her.

Adeline pulls cash from her small purse and hands over a five. "Keep it," she says, and then picks four fresh peaches from the top of the pile. The woman at the table holds a paper sack open, and once Adeline has her new treasures placed inside, we continue on our way.

"I thought Georgia was the peach state," she quips, casually grinning as we stroll through the market.

"You think peaches only grow in Georgia?"

She shakes her head. "No, I know they don't, but these are so big and beautiful, you'd think they come straight from one of their huge orchards."

We walk a little farther until we reach the end and then turn to hit the booths on the opposite side of the walkway. Adeline stops to check the goods at nearly every single stand along the way, but it doesn't bother me. In fact, I find her excitement at the little things a breath of fresh air. She compliments nearly every vendor on something at their stand, and always paid more than they were asking. I find I've had a smile on my face pretty much the entire morning, and though it's a little unusual, I go with it. I'd much rather spend the day smiling with Adeline than not.

"That was the best," she confirms after we finish visiting the final booth.

"I'm glad you enjoyed it. I like coming here on the weekends. There's always something for everyone."

She glances down at the bags I'm carrying. "Or in my case, a lot of somethings for everyone." She cringes a little before adding, "There was just so much stuff to see. So much time and energy went into selling their wares, and I felt it necessary to show my support for their efforts."

"You don't have to explain yourself. I've bought plenty of things I probably didn't necessarily need over the last nine or ten months."

She grins and reaches for the flowers, bringing them to her nose. "I know the resort has fresh flowers everywhere, but I thought these would be lovely in my room."

I nod in confirmation as we make our way to where my car is parked in the large lot. "They will. In fact, all the flowers they purchase are from local vendors like that."

"Wow, that's neat. I assumed they used a florist."

"They do at times, but not always."

Adeline slides into the seat after I place all our bags in the back. The moment I climb into the driver's seat, she leans back on the headrest and sighs in contentment. "What's next?"

"Well, I thought we could drive down the coast for a bit and grab a bite to eat."

"Perfect," she replies. "Should we take my loot back to the resort?"

"We could, or we could drop it off at my place, since it's closer. Then pick it back up on our ride back."

She didn't buy anything requiring refrigeration, but with the flowers and peaches, those probably shouldn't be left in a hot car all afternoon. "Perfect," she answers.

We get lucky Marian isn't outside when we arrive, so that shaves a little extra time off the stop. Soon, we're driving down the coast, windows down and soaking up the gorgeous Florida sun. I find myself having a hard time keeping my eyes on the road. I'm drawn to the way her hair blows in the breeze and her lips hold a constant happy little grin. She seems perfectly content to sit there, enjoying something as simple as taking a cruise.

"What's that?" she asks, pointing out at the ocean.

I glance out and spot the odd boat she's referring to. "That's a dolphin watching boat."

"Seriously?" she asks, her eyes widening. "I've heard about those tours but never been."

"No?" I ask, my brain already starting to spin with an idea.

She shakes her head. "I've been fortunate to visit some of the most beautiful places in the world, but we were never allowed to join tours. Mother felt it was beneath us," she mutters.

I don't miss the sadness etched on her face before she quickly looks away, trying to hide it. "I'm sorry."

She waves off my apology, her eyes drawn back out to the passing boat. "It's all right. Like I've said, I've seen some amazing locations in my life."

Shrugging, I follow her eyes for a moment before returning them to the roadway. "Seeing the beauty is one thing, but experiencing what it has to offer is on a whole different level."

Adeline nods, as if understanding me completely. "Someday," she whispers, closing her eyes and angling her face just enough to allow the warm air to wash over her. "Someday, I'll experience all that life has to offer and not just watch it slip by."

Reaching over, I take her hand in mine, and we spend the next twenty minutes driving in silence. It never feels uncomfortable or stilted. It's two individuals enjoying the scenery surrounding them and being in the moment.

When we slow down, she sits up in the seat, her blue eyes sparkling with anticipation. "Where are we?"

"Spring Harbor. It's about an hour south of the resort," I reply, pulling into the first parking spot I find along the main downtown street.

"What are we doing here?" she asks eagerly, already releasing her seat belt.

"Well, there's a great seafood place on the water. It's always packed, so it'll take a while to get a table, but that's okay. They have things to do while we wait."

I'm drawn to those damn sapphire orbs like a moth to a flame. "What kind of things?"

Opening my door, I glance her way and smile. "Come on, I'll show you."

She extends her hand, which I readily take, as we head in the direction of the beach restaurant. As we approach, I try to see the area through her eyes. It's not just a restaurant. It's a small village. There are shops, beach volleyball pits, miniature golf, and even Frisbee golf available to enjoy while you wait to eat.

"Wow," she mutters, stopping in her tracks when we reach the sand.

"Right? I'll never forget the first time I was here. I stumbled upon it actually. I was having a shit day and just started driving. Discovered this place and sort of fell in love with it. I come down about once a month," I tell her, leading her toward the restaurant first.

She doesn't say a word as we head for the hostess stand. "Good afternoon. How many?" the young girl asks.

"Two, please."

The young lady types on the screen. "It's about an hour to an hour and fifteen-minute wait."

"No problem," I assure her, understanding the program.

"Last name, please?"

"Paulson." I give her my cell phone number as soon as she asks.

"Perfect. You'll receive a text message when your table is ready."

"Great," I reply before leading Adeline back outside. "So, what shall we do first?"

"Well, I haven't played volleyball since PE in school and never in the sand or with a dress, so maybe we should avoid that?"

I chuckle. "Probably a good idea."

"How about miniature golf? I've never played."

I'm unable to mask my shock. "Really? Never?" When she shakes her head, I move in that direction. "You're in for a treat."

"I don't know about that. I've never been very sporty."

"Two, please," I say to the high schooler working the counter where we'll get our golf balls and clubs. "You don't have to be sporty," I reassure her, handing the young man cash to play. When he returns my change, I point over to the bucket of clubs in a variety of colors. "Pick your club, madam."

She chooses a pink one and is handed a matching pink ball, while I stick with blue. Not because it's a boy color, but for the simple fact it reminds me of her eyes and I seem to be a little obsessed with them.

When we reach the first hole, I point to the place where she will tee off. "You'll have to tell me how to do this," she insists, depositing the ball on the small tee.

"It's easy. You don't need a lot of power, so don't swing high," I tell her, watching as she stands awkwardly beside the tee. "Want me to show you?"

"Yes, please," she replies, taking a step to move away.

I stop her though, gently pulling her back. When she realizes I'm going to position her body and help her swing, she relaxes in my arms and allows me to put her in the correct position. "Like this," I say softly, carefully swinging her arms back and then moving the club forward until she hits the ball.

"Oh!" she bellows excitedly when the ball nearly lands in the hole. "That's not so bad," she adds, looking back at me over her shoulder.

"It's not," I agree, placing a kiss on her bare shoulder. "You got it?" I ask, starting to pull away.

"It may take me a few more swings to get the hang of it," she quips, her blue eyes dancing with mirth.

I chuckle, realizing what she's doing and approving wholeheartedly. "Yeah? Maybe I should help you for a few more strokes."

"Strokes," she replies with a giggle. She shifts her hips, sliding her firm ass against my cock. If he wasn't hard and ready before, he definitely is now, and all it took was the slightest touch.

"Don't be naughty, Miss Montgomery. There are children present," I tease, nipping at her shoulder with my teeth.

She gasps, and I'm not sure if it's from the bite or the families nearby. "Then you should most definitely stop grinding your erection against me," she mutters. "It puts thoughts in my head."

I laugh, low and gravelly. "Thoughts? I think I'd like to know them."

She smirks before sashaying toward her ball. "I think I'd rather show you."

My cock kicks with excitement in my shorts, and I curse myself for not wearing underwear. I hate them and rarely have them on. I should have really thought more about having her near though, because it's much harder to conceal an erection in khaki shorts without that extra layer of support.

Holding my hands in front of myself, I turn to watch a young boy and girl play a few holes over, as well as an older couple right behind them. It does exactly what I was hoping it would do, and within a few minutes, I'm under control once more.

"Ready to play?" she asks, humor laced in each word.

"I'm ready," I confirm, not going into detail about what exactly I'm ready for. The last thing I need is to pop another boner right here in the middle of the mini-golf course.

We finish playing nine of the eighteen holes and choose to spend the rest of our wait for our table over at the seaside shops. In the first one, she finds homemade taffy in a variety of flavors. "I've never had taffy."

"What?" I ask, reaching for a medium-sized bag. "Here. Pick your flavors."

Her eyes roam over the dozens of varieties of chewy candy. "There are so many options." I stand by and watch as she takes her time choosing pieces of candy for her bag, considering each and every flavor. "Which one is your favorite?"

"I love the key lime pie," I tell her.

Adeline scoops a few extras of that flavor into her bag, and when it's finally full, she zips it closed and smiles. I take her hand in mine as we browse the other items on our way to the front counter. I spot a display of handmade jewelry at the same time she does. "Look at this. Isn't it gorgeous?"

Without answering, I reach for the necklace that catches my eye. It's a circular sterling silver pendant with a wave through the middle, but it's what is beneath that wave that catches my attention.

"That's made with real sand from the beach outside and crushed blue sea glass," the older woman behind the counter announces. "My daughter is the jewelry maker," she adds proudly.

"It's beautiful," Adeline insists, tracing the pendant with the tip of her finger.

"I want to buy this for you."

Her wide eyes fly up to meet mine. "What? That's not necessary."

"I insist," I state, releasing the clasp and pulling the necklace from the display piece of cardboard. She doesn't say a word as I move to place it around her neck and secure it.

The necklace hits perfectly against her skin. "It's beautiful."

"Something to commemorate your week of independence."

Her eyes fire to life as they fill with tears. "I wouldn't forget my time here without the necklace."

I lean forward and kiss the tip of her nose. "Now you'll be able to take a piece of Florida home with you."

She nods, and if she wants to argue about the purchase of the necklace, she doesn't. In reality, it's an inexpensive piece. For less than forty dollars, she's able to take a beautiful trinket home with her at the end of our time together. It doesn't go unnoticed she's wearing brilliant diamonds in her ears and has a delicate diamond and sapphire ring on her right hand. Those pieces cost far more than the one I'm gifting her, but it's not about the money. It's the sentiment, and I know she realizes it too.

My phone vibrates in my pocket. "That's our cue."

"Good," she replies, grinning widely and blinking away the wetness in her eyes. "I'm starved. Let's go eat."

Chapter NINE

Adeline

"Are you serious?" I ask, my mouth probably hanging open in shock.

Decker laughs. "Yes."

I gaze at the boat docked at the marina and back at the man sitting in the driver's seat. The sun is shining high above our heads, the late morning Monday air warm and inviting just outside the car. I can't help but look back and forth between the two, unable to comprehend how someone can continually be so amazing.

Decker Paulson is a remarkable person. Yes, I understand I've known him a matter of days, but in that short time, he's proven to be incredibly considerate, watchful, and thoughtful. I've spent the last two nights with him in my bed, and both nights have been incredible. I've had more orgasms in less than forty-eight hours than I have in the last two years.

Now, he's booked us on a dolphin watching adventure, and I couldn't be more thrilled.

"Come on, Addi. We have a boat to catch," he says, getting out of his car and meeting me around at the passenger side door like usual. He retrieves the beach bag he packed from the back seat, takes my hand, and escorts me toward the marina office.

It takes a few minutes to fill out the information requested and sign the waiver that proclaims them not liable for a whole slew of personal problems—including death—and then we join the rest of the group who'll enjoy today's dolphin watching trip. When it's time to board the boat, I'm practically vibrating with excitement.

The crew proceeds to move through their safety instructions, handing out life jackets to anyone requesting one and the kids on the boat who are required to wear one. Decker and I opt to not wear one during the trip but know they are just beneath our seats if we decide to put them on.

Decker places the bag between his feet, and my eyes peruse his casual appearance. He's wearing brightly colored swim trunks, a fitted gray T-shirt, and for the first time since I've met him, a pair of black flip-flops. He has a ball cap on his head and a pair of sunglasses on his face, and his overall vibe is very laid-back and relaxed.

At his insistence this morning, I'm wearing a bikini beneath one of my more casual sundresses. My feet are stuffed in a pair of blue and tan flip-flops I purchased at the resort gift shop, since all my footwear were brought with wedding activities in mind. I have on my own big sunglasses and am wishing I would have thought to bring my floppy hat. Even though there's an awning over the boat, the sun is still brutal and reflecting off every metal surface and the water surrounding us.

"Here," Decker says, handing over the bottle of sunscreen he grabbed from my room. "The sun will be pretty intense out on the water."

I start to cover my arms with the sunscreen, and quickly turn my attention to my face, legs, and feet. When it's time to cover my back and shoulders, Decker takes the bottle and squirts a glob into his palm. His warm hands are almost electrifying as they glide across my shoulders, his fingers slipping beneath the thin straps of my bikini top and the sundress. The way my nipples harden at his touch reminds me of how he helped me take off my dress last night when we got back to my room. Very slowly and very meticulously, and it was followed up with two orgasms.

"Stop it," he mutters, kissing the top of my neck at my hairline.

"I didn't do anything," I murmur.

He chuckles, his fingers flexing against my skin. "No, but you were thinking it."

I gently lift my shoulder. "Maybe," I respond coyly, feeling a blush burn my cheeks.

He kisses the back of my head once and whispers, "Me too, Addi.

Me too." Then, he begins to spread sunscreen over his own legs, face, and arms. When it's time to remove his T-shirt, my mouth goes dry at the incredibly fit and gorgeous man before me.

I reach for the sunscreen and return the favor, slathering up his back, sides, and shoulders with the sunblock because I need to have my hands on him. "Want me to get your chest?" I quip, knowing he's perfectly capable.

"Hell no. You put your hands on me again, and I'll never get my hard-on down," he whispers.

Grateful there's no one sitting directly beside us, I grin mischievously at his obvious discomfort. "Hang on a bit, and I'll help you with that problem later."

He snorts a laugh. "I'll be looking forward to it."

Relaxing in our seats, Decker places his arm around my shoulder as we set off for our adventure. There are a couple of kids anxiously bouncing in their seats, eyes already scanning the water for the first sight of a dolphin. While I'm equally as excited as they are, I'm drawn to their enthusiasm and wide toothy grins.

"Is your phone in your purse?" he asks as we head out to a popular destination for dolphin spotting.

"Oh, I didn't bring it," I confess, knowing it's still back in my room on the table. The truth is, since I sent my emails Saturday evening, I haven't turned it on. I know what's waiting for me if I do. The anger, the accusations, the threats. They'll be in black and white the moment I boot up my cellular device, and frankly, I'm tired. I'm tired of living a life the way someone else dictates. I'm tired of not being me, but what I fear the most is having no idea who that person even is.

He looks like he wants to ask questions, but he doesn't. Just nods once and pulls his own phone from the pocket of his swim trunks. "No worries, Adeline. I have mine to document our trip." Decker taps across the screen and holds it up in front of us. He leans over and says, "Smile," before snapping a few pictures on his phone. Then, we turn our full attention to the water and beauty that surrounds us.

Over the next hour, we spot several dolphins jumping in the ocean, and I find Decker snapping a few pictures every now and again. I even see the phone pointed at me a time or two, but don't say anything. By the time the boat is pulling back into the marina, I'm smiling from ear to ear and exhausted at the same time.

What an adventure.

We walk from the boat hand in hand toward the parking lot. "Thank you so much for that. It was simply amazing," I say, pausing when we reach his car and placing a kiss on his cheek.

He squeezes my hand. "You're very welcome."

"What now?" I ask when he opens the door for me to slide in.

"Well, I have a staff meeting in a little bit that'll probably take an hour or so. Maybe afterward, we can make plans for dinner." He crouches down in the open doorway of the car, a worried look on his face. "Unless you have something else to do. I don't want to monopolize all your free time. I could just as easily get a few things done at my place during the day and come over at night."

My throat is tight with the reminder of what this really is.

A hookup.

A vacation hookup in which both parties will go their separate ways soon.

Yet, despite the reminder, it still feels different. I enjoy spending time with him, even if our time together has been short.

Knowing I can't spend every moment of every day with him, I say, "I've been thinking about having another massage at the spa. Perhaps I'll check their availability when we get back to the resort."

He nods. "I've heard they're fantastic," he replies, standing up and preparing to shut the door.

"Never had one?" I ask before he can accomplish the task.

"Not from there. I had one a few years ago from a girl I was seeing," he states with a wicked smile.

A bubble of laughter slips from my lips. "Something tells me there wasn't much massaging going on there."

He chuckles low and dirty. "Oh, there was some massaging happening, but I don't think it was in the traditional sense." With a wink, he shuts the door and walks around to the driver's door.

The moment he's inside and has the car started, I ask, "You work tomorrow evening, right?"

"Yep. Four to midnight tomorrow and Wednesday. I'm filling in for someone at the tiki bar by the pool on Thursday from eleven to four, off Friday, and then four to two on Saturday."

"How about we play it by ear. Maybe we can meet up for dinner tonight. I do have a bit of thanking you in store for today's tour."

He glances over at me, pulling his sunglasses down a bit, and meeting my gaze. "Yeah? That sounds like a special thank-you."

"Oh, it is," I reply coyly, looking forward at the traffic passing by.

He doesn't say a word as he pulls from the lot onto the highway that runs along the coast, but he doesn't have to. I can tell by the outline in his trunks that he has an erection, and that gives me a bit of an ego boost.

"Perhaps after dinner we can order dessert. To go. Rumor has it, the strawberries and whipped cream are divine."

Decker groans, reaching down and adjusting his crotch. "You're a wicked woman."

With a shrug, I'm unable to keep the smile off my lips as I say, "You bring it out of me."

"Hmm," he says, tapping his thumb on the steering wheel. "What exactly did you have in mind with your dessert, Addi?" His voice is husky and raw, and it makes my core slick with desire.

I turn his way, my eyebrows drawn together in curiosity. "You need me to explain it to you?" I tease.

"No, I just want to hear you say the words."

Clearing my throat, I ignore my need to shy away from speaking my truth. This week is about finding that person who has been buried away and allow her to emerge. That means not holding back on things I feel, things I want. "Well, I was really hoping to use a little bit of that whipped cream on you and lick it off."

His eyes are wide. Even through the dark sunglasses, I can see the whites of his eyes. "Say the words, Addi. Tell me you want to lick it off my cock."

Swallowing hard, I inhale slowly and say, "I want to cover your cock in whipped cream, Decker, and slowly lick every drop off."

He groans again, this one laced with agony. "Jesus, your mouth is magic. Just hearing you say the word cock has me so hard, I can barely think straight."

"Well, as long as you can still drive straight."

He chuckles once and shakes his head. Before I know it, we're pulling into the parking lot of the resort. He drives around to the back of the building where the employees park. Neither of us says a word as he retrieves the bag from the back seat and meets me at the passenger door. Then, he takes my hand again and leads me around the building to the front entrance.

The air-conditioning is welcome and cool as the doors slide open and we step inside. I don't really know what my plan is, but I wouldn't mind taking him back to my room and starting our whipped cream thank-you a bit early. Unfortunately, that's halted the moment we pass the front desk.

"Miss Montgomery," the older gentleman says, grabbing my attention. "I have a message for you."

A heaviness settles in my chest. "A message?"

"Yes, ma'am." He holds out a piece of paper, and it takes all the strength I have to walk in his direction and accept it. A part of me wants to keep moving, to ignore the slip of paper in his hand. I already know who it's from, and I shouldn't be surprised he has resorted to contacting me this way. My father hates to be ignored, and that's exactly what I've been doing since I sent my email and turned off my phone.

"Thank you," I reply, accepting the message and hoping my words sound stronger than I feel. A blush creeps up my neck at the thought of this man having to write down the words my father said. I'm sure they are vile, condescending, and quite rude. Words he wouldn't use if he were standing here at the counter. No, that's not true either. He'd no doubt use those words, but they'd be directed at me and not the innocent resort employee who was unfortunate enough to answer the call.

"You're most welcome. Enjoy your stay." He gives me a smile, but it seems to hold nothing but sincerity.

For that, I'm grateful.

Decker walks beside me as I move toward the elevator. The slip of paper in my hand burns my fingers, and I know I need to be alone when I read it. "Listen, why don't I go up to my room alone. You have your meeting soon, and I might need to lie down for a while to recoup from our water excursion."

He stares at me for several moments before nodding slowly. "Of course. A nap is always on the schedule when you're on vacation," he replies diplomatically.

"Yes."

He reaches out and presses the call button for the elevator. "Don't forget to call down to the spa."

I nod. "I will do that."

He hands me the beach bag, which contains a few of my things. "I'll check on you later," he replies just as the elevator door opens.

"Sounds good." I step inside the car and try to give him a warm smile, but even I can tell it doesn't reach my eyes.

Decker hesitates but doesn't say a word. Just presses the button for my floor and takes a step out of the car. "See you soon, Adeline."

"Thank you, again, Decker."

He nods as the door closes, and I'm left alone in the ascending elevator car. My heart is pounding, and even though I should look at the message still clenched in my hand, I know I need to wait until I'm tucked away in my room. If I'm going to react, I'd rather do it alone.

I slip easily into my room and lock the door behind me. I place the bag on the bed and walk to the sliding patio door overlooking the ocean. The warm breeze heats my skin as it wraps around me, but the comfort it once held only a short time ago is void. Sighing, I walk over to the side of the bed and take a seat. Only then do I open the folded paper in my hand.

Adeline,

I hope you are enjoying your time away. I was able to reschedule the dinner with Jefferson for this Sunday. I hope that works for you. I'd feel terrible if we had to reschedule again. The Martin family's time is so limited, and there are pressing matters to discuss. He looks forward to spending time with you and finalizing the agreement.

Five o'clock. Morticia's Steakhouse.

Edward Montgomery

P.S.: Let's have your phone looked at when you return. It seems to be having difficulties accepting and making phone calls.

I let out a very unladylike snort as I finish his message. *Edward Montgomery*. As if the message could have been from anyone else. Even if he used the word Dad—which he never does—I'd know it was from him.

I reread it again, rolling my eyes at the underlying message. To someone casually reading it—or to a man taking the note—you might think this was a normal message, but it's not. There's a hidden meaning in every sentence, one I'm fluent in speaking. He's telling me under no uncertain terms am I to miss Sunday dinner, that the plan for me to date and eventually marry Jefferson Martin is still happening.

And let's not forget about his P.S. That's his demand I turn my phone on, and while I almost get up and grab the device, I force myself to set the paper down and walk to the balcony. The afternoon sun is shining high in the sky, reflecting off the water in gorgeous shades of blues and greens, and the sand sparkles like gorgeous ivory crystals. If I look to my right, I can see the side of the pool area. While I've checked it out, I have yet to enjoy that part of the resort.

Instead of taking a nap or resting while Decker is at his meeting, I step back in the room and shut the sliding door. With a smile on my face, I lift my sundress over my head and grab the blue sheer cover-up, that really does nothing to actually cover anything up. I slip my keycard in my bag Decker had packed earlier, slip a new beach towel inside, and head for the door without glancing at the note still sitting on the bed.

With my head held high, I exit my room and prepare to enjoy the pool area for a while. This is a vacation, right? I might as well enjoy myself while I can. Everything else will still be there when I'm ready to face it.

Chapter TEN

Decker

The group who assembled in the employee break room starts to exit the large space. Some are off to start their shifts, while others head down the hall that leads to the parking lot. Since I'm off work for the day, I'd normally follow the latter out of the building, but I can't stop thinking about Adeline. Something definitely upset her about that message she received, and while I wanted to press the matter, I didn't really feel it was my place. We've been acquainted a matter of days.

However, I can't get over the feeling deep in my gut telling me I should have pressed the issue. What if she's in trouble? I could at least ask about it, make sure there isn't something darker causing those rain clouds in her gorgeous blue eyes. I trust Adeline is single, but what if there's a crazy ex she's dealing with? Has someone tracked her down to the resort, someone's she's trying to stay away from? It would explain why she's keeping her phone off.

Unable to get past the uneasiness in my gut, I know I need to go to her room and talk to her. If she doesn't want to tell me, that's fine, but I have to try. I can't help her if I don't know she's in trouble.

I plan to make my way up to her room when one of the cabana guys comes in smiling. "Damn, I love when foxes stay at the resort. They definitely make the day go a lot better," he says, catching the attention of not only myself, but two other employees too.

"She single?" the younger guy who recently started asks. He's a part-time cabana guy, helping set up the outdoor areas each morning or taking them down at night. They also offer to retrieve drinks or food orders for guests so they don't have to leave their personal paradise. I think his name is James, but since I haven't actually worked with him, I'm not a hundred percent sure.

Deacon, the cabana guy on shift today, smiles. "And fucking smokin' hot. Tall, leggy, and wearing this tiny little blue and pink bikini."

A smile spreads across my face because I already know who he's referring to.

"Blonde, right?" Clinton asks. He's the one I'm working for tomorrow in the tiki bar by the pool. His newborn daughter has a doctor's appointment he doesn't want to miss.

"Yep," Deacon replies with a mischievous grin. Not that I blame him. Adeline *is* smokin' hot, and if I were out there, I'd probably be tripping over my tongue with drool all down the front of my shirt too.

"She was with that wedding that didn't happen on Saturday. One of the bridesmaids. I remember seeing her a handful of times around the resort," Clinton adds before slowly turning my way. "Actually, I think I've heard she's staying the week." He doesn't say anything else, but I can feel his eyes bore into the side of my head.

"Damn, I wouldn't mind hitting that while she's here," Deacon boasts, and before I can stop myself, I snort a laugh. "What?" he asks, puffing out his chest a little.

"Nothing," I reply, leaning against the wall and refusing to give him anything.

"Dude, ain't no way you're hitting that," the younger guy replies with a laugh. "She's already hitting it with Decker."

I should be surprised by his comment, but I'm not. This resort isn't *that* big. The first night I went up to her room, it was under camera surveillance. Any employee could have seen us leave together yesterday or today. We haven't exactly been hiding it, though not flaunting it either.

"What the hell, man!" Deacon hollers. "You're sleeping with the hot blonde? And not sharing deets?"

I just stare at him.

The young guy laughs at Deacon. "You didn't know? That was all everyone was talking about last night when I was getting ready to leave work. Apparently, they spent the day together and he went to her room last night."

Clinton sighs and shakes his head. "Kid, don't fall for all the crap you hear around here. Rule number one: Ninety percent of what you hear is going to be gossip."

The young guy's mouth falls open. "It's not gossip!" He turns to face me. "Right?"

I shrug, refusing to speak.

Clinton laughs, slapping the younger guy on the back. "Rule number two: Don't brag."

"If I was bangin' the blonde, I'd totally brag," Deacon mutters. Finally, he sighs and shakes his head. "Well, since I've already lost half of my break talking to you assholes, I'm going to run back and grab a quick drink and bite to eat. Talk to you soon." He starts to walk toward the employee break room we all just vacated. "Oh, and, Deck? You let me know when you're done with the blonde, all right?" He flashes me a wolfish grin before slipping inside the room, disappearing from the hallway.

I don't even realize my hands are balled into fists until Clinton places his hand on my arm. "Let it go. We both know he's all talk and doesn't actually have a chance with her. Hell, he knows it too. He's just trying to get under your skin now that he knows you're hanging with her."

I nod, forcing myself to relax again.

"Sorry, Decker. I wasn't trying to start stuff," the younger guy says, a look of remorse on his face.

"It's all right," I tell him. "What's your name?"

"Matt. I just started a few weeks ago."

"Well, Matt, keep out of all the gossip bullshit and you'll be fine. You'll hear a lot of shit on the job, probably see stuff you shouldn't repeat too. The housekeeping staff is probably the worst with gossip, but bartenders aren't much better. You know the rules. Follow them and do your job. What you do on the side, off the clock, is your business."

Matt nods, drinking in my every word. "I understand. I won't say anything about you and the blonde, but I'm certain almost everyone already knows. I even heard a few people talking about it when you walked into the meeting."

I sigh. "Well, I'm not doing anything wrong. She's a guest, but anything we do happens when I'm off the clock. We're both single and adults."

"Got it. Okay, I gotta head out. You guys have a good afternoon," Matt says, walking toward the rear entrance of the building.

"You may not know this, but my girlfriend, DeeDee? She was a guest here when I met her," Clinton says when we're left alone in the hallway.

"Yeah?"

He nods with a smile. "Yeah. She was somewhat local but staying here for a girls' weekend trip. She and four other friends were hanging out at the pool, and she was the most beautiful woman I'd ever seen. I couldn't help but flirt," he says with a chuckle.

"When I found out she lived only about twenty minutes away, I asked her out. I couldn't believe it when she said yes."

I feel my own smile spreading across my lips, matching his.

"We've been together almost two years, and our baby girl, Amelia, was born three months ago. I plan to marry that woman one day," he adds.

"Good for you."

"All I'm saying is sometimes you meet crappy human beings in this line of work, but other times you meet the person who changes your life."

I want to tell him it's just a fling, that there are no pretenses about happily ever afters or forevers, but I keep my mouth shut. I'm not embarrassed by the word *fling*, but I also don't really feel it's accurate. Adeline may be someone I'm sleeping with for the time being, but she's quickly becoming a friend too. I enjoy talking to her and spending time with her outside of the bed.

"I better head home. DeeDee's working tonight, so I only have a little time with her and Amelia together before she leaves for the hospital," he states, turning and walking away. Before he leaves, he says, "Thanks for working for me tomorrow. Let me know when I can return the favor."

I nod and am left alone in the hall only moments later. I realize quickly I'd rather be near her. I should definitely give her alone time to soak up the sun at the pool, but for whatever reason, my legs carry me in that direction. The sun is hot outside, the sounds of fun, upbeat music coming from the small stage. The pool is busy, several of the lounge chairs just outside the fence on the beach also in use. Even during the week, the resort stays pretty busy.

It only takes me a second to spot Adeline. She's a vision of pure beauty and elegance, even lying in the sun. Her hair is pulled back in a tight ponytail, and she has those big, expensive sunglasses on her face. Her entire body looks sun-kissed, her vibrant blue and pink bikini only accentuating the bronze coloring of her skin.

I watch as a man passing by practically trips over himself when he spots her and does a double take, and I can't help but chuckle. Adeline has this exotic way of drawing you in, even if she's not trying to.

My feet start moving in her direction before I register the action. I stop when I reach her chair, my shadow falling across her body. "Good day, Miss Montgomery. I hope you're resting well this afternoon."

The slightest smile tickles her lips. She reaches up, pulling those big sunglasses down her nose and gazing up at me from beneath her lashes. "Ahh, hello, Mr....Paulson, is it?"

Hands on my hips, I tsk and shake my head. "Just Decker, ma'am. Are you enjoying the gorgeous afternoon?"

She smirks, dragging her eyes slowly down my body before she answers. "The view is quite remarkable."

I chuckle at her blatant flirting and feel my dick twitch in my shorts. "It is," I agree, my eyes drinking her in from head to toe.

Finding the lounge chair on her left empty, I take a seat, facing her. "Big plans later?"

Adeline shrugs casually. "Well, I was thinking about that just a few minutes ago. I believe room service is on the menu this evening."

My dick doesn't just twitch this time but starts to get fully hard. "Yeah? Planning to stay in your room all evening?"

"Yes. A friend I met recently did an incredible thing for me today, and I've been planning all the ways I want to thank him."

Yeah. No way am I walking out of the pool area anytime soon. "Tell me more," I insist, placing my elbows on my knees and leaning forward.

"Well, someone told me the dinner special for this evening is a lobster ravioli that sounds divine. I thought perhaps my new friend and I can order dinner." She meets my gaze as she adds, "*And* dessert." She pushes her glasses back up on the bridge of her nose and gives a satisfied little smirk, as if she knows exactly what her words are doing to me.

"Speaking of your new friend," I start, keeping my voice low enough that no one should be able to hear our conversation. "I have it on good authority that the cat is out of the bag."

It's in that moment Deacon returns from his break and spots me sitting beside Adeline. His knowing smile is wide as he passes by and heads to the bar to retrieve a tray to continue serving drinks.

"I see," she replies. "Well, my friend and I weren't exactly hiding our time together. Is it an issue?"

"No," I quickly reassure her. "Your friend just has to maintain a professional exchange while he's working."

She leans back against the chair and looks up at the sun, as if soaking in its heat. "I'm sure my friend will maintain his profession-alism when necessary. Any other time, well, I hope he's a bit more… uninhibited. I rather enjoy that side of him."

Yeah, my cock could cut glass right now it's so rigid and ready to show her exactly how uninhibited I am. Instead, I just smile, silently vowing to give her exactly what she's requesting later this evening when we're alone.

After a few minutes of silence in the sun, I spot a woman approach-ing, her eyes on me. "Excuse me," she says gently. "I believe you're in my seat."

Wishing I didn't have to get up so soon, I carefully stand, glad my erection isn't at full attention anymore. "Well, I apologize completely," I state, stepping back so the woman can have her seat.

"This is Reece Jones. She's staying at the resort this week," Adeline announces to me.

"Reece, happy to make your acquaintance," I reply, extending my hand.

The pretty woman places hers in mine and gives it a gentle shake. "You must be Decker."

I'm able to school my surprise, but barely. "I am."

When she releases my hand, Reece takes a seat in the lounge chair beside Adeline. "I invited Adeline to join me for dinner this evening, but she already has plans." The woman smiles, glancing my way over her own sunglasses. "I can definitely see why," she adds, making me laugh.

"Reece is here with her husband, who is golfing in the tournament nearby," Adeline confirms, taking a sip of what looks like water.

"And you're not there, cheering him on?" I ask.

"Are you kidding? Golf has to be the most boring, dreadful sport in the history of all activities. I don't understand it at all, but Nathanial loves it, so I support his passions. And he supports mine by allowing me to tag along on some of his golf trips and spend his money in the spa and with little shopping trips," Reece states with a chuckle.

"We've agreed to have dinner tomorrow night instead," Adeline states.

"Yes, tomorrow." Reece once again looks my way. "Then she can give me all the dirty details from her plans this evening."

I bark out a laugh and watch Adeline blush.

"There will be no detail sharing," Adeline insists, shaking her head at her new friend's antics.

"You say that now, but after a martini or two, you'll be singing his praises for all to hear. Trust me. Nathanial and I have been married for nearly thirteen years, but you'd think it's been thirteen weeks. We're happily in the honeymoon phase, and I do love to share."

Adeline and I make eye contact, and I get this weird feeling in the pit of my gut. Suddenly, Reece bursts out laughing. "Oh my God, your faces. I don't mean sharing like *sharing*. I just meant I love to overshare about the size of Nathanial's nine iron, if you know what I mean. I'm way too possessive to share. His club is mine alone. I don't share."

Shaking my head, I find myself laughing at this slightly loud, completely crazy woman. And I mean crazy in a good way. She seems fun, and I hope Adeline is able to unwind and enjoy her time with her.

"All right, ladies. I'll let you get back to it. I'm sure I'll see you around."

"Oh, you'll definitely be seeing one of us later," Reece quips.

With a chuckle, I turn to make my exit when Adeline stops me. "Decker?" I pause and glance back over my shoulder to meet her gaze. "Any time after six."

Nodding, I walk away with a little extra spring in my step.

At six oh five, I lift my hand and knock on the door. Adeline opens it immediately, reaching for my arm and pulling me inside. The moment the door is closed, she's on me, my back pressed against the door and her mouth covering mine. My arms wrap around her, trying to draw her closer, my hands gripping her ass. "Well, this is quite the welcome," I'm able to get out as she moves her mouth to my jaw and down my neck.

"Naked, Decker. Get naked. Now." She punctuates her demand by biting my chin.

"Yes, ma'am," I state, holding her ass and lifting.

Adeline squeals, her legs wrapping around my waist. "Put me down. I'm too big for this."

"You may be tall, but you are in no way too big, Addi. You're absolutely fucking perfect," I insist, depositing her gently onto the bed. Then, I get to work removing my shorts and T-shirt.

Her eyes follow my every move, especially when I drop my shorts. "God, I love the fact you don't wear underwear."

"Maybe you should do away with them too," I state, waggling my eyebrows suggestively.

"I already have," she replies casually, making my dick even harder.

"You're not wearing panties, Adeline?"

"Nope." She pops the P and licks her lips. "Want me to show you?"

Reaching for my wallet, I pull a condom out and walk over to the chaise lounge. Finally, I wave my hand. "Please."

She stands up and moves toward me, stopping just out of my reach. I take in her appearance. Adeline's wearing a silky black tank top with large flowers on it. The top is loose and flowy and doesn't reveal what prizes she's concealing beneath it. She releases the tiny zipper at her armpit and slowly removes the top. Her perky tits are on full display, the outline from her bikini apparent on her tanned skin.

"I see you got a little sun today," I note, my eyes devouring her hard nipples and perfect tits.

"I did," she confirms, releasing the button and zipper on the tan shorts she's wearing. "I have tan lines," she adds, dropping the shorts.

"Hmm," I reply, twisting my finger so she spins around. "I'm going to have to inspect these tan lines."

Painfully slow, she turns, exposing her beautiful ass for me to see. Glancing over her shoulder, she whispers, "Good. I'm afraid I can't see the ones behind me. I definitely need your expertise."

Expertise.

She wants it?

She's got it.

Chapter ELEVEN

Adeline

Decker reaches for the condom and sheathes his erection within seconds. "Come here."

Smiling, I take a single step in his direction, knowing he can't quite reach me yet. "Well, I was hoping I'd be able to thank you properly for the tour we did today," I insist, my eyes dropping to his impressive erection.

"Later," he grunts out, tossing the foil package onto the floor. "Right now, I need to fuck you, Addi. Now. Hard and fast. That okay?"

My response is to finish stepping his way and climbing onto the chair. I place each knee at his sides and lower myself down to hover above him. He must sense exactly what's on my mind, because he reaches down and holds his erection, guiding me down until I feel him starting to fill me. Then, I lower myself completely, and our combined moans of pleasure fill the room.

Decker lets me set the pace as I adjust to his size, but that control is short-lived. He places his hands on the sides of my rear and lifts, bringing me back down with a bit of force. My legs start to burn, but I ignore it. The gratification far exceeds any discomfort I may feel in my muscles.

"Jesus," he mutters, my body starting to move on its own. He thrusts up each time I slam down, and the result is pure bliss.

I cry out, my release already building in epic fashion. Holding on to his shoulders, I continue to lift myself up and drop back down. I've never had sex in this position, but I'm already a big fan, and I haven't even had an orgasm yet. But I can tell he'll deliver spectacularly.

Without breaking his stride, he asks, "Tell me you're close, Addi."

"So close," I mutter, gripping the hard muscles of his shoulders.

He continues to thrust upward, hitting all the right places and sending me into orbit in a matter of seconds. The orgasm consumes me, spreading through my veins like fire, devouring every part of me and leaving me breathless. Decker groans, pauses for a second, and then follows me over the edge. He moves his hips, riding out his own release, taking what he needs.

When we both fall boneless onto the chair, our bodies are slick with sweat and our breathing is heavy. That doesn't stop him from running his lips up my neck and nibbling on my earlobe. "That was some hello," he whispers, nuzzling his nose against my skin.

"Mmm," I mumble, practically singing with bliss. "Now I'm hungry."

I feel his chest vibrate with his chuckle. "Lobster ravioli, right?"

"Have you had it?" I ask, pulling back to look at him.

"I have. It's one of my favorites," he assures me. "Why don't I go take care of the condom. We can both clean up a little and call room service. It's a beautiful night. We can eat on the balcony."

"That sounds perfect," I state, gingerly climbing off his lap. My legs are a bit wobbly, but I'd do it all over again.

When he stands, he stops in front of me and kisses my forehead. "You okay? I didn't hurt you?"

"Hurt me?" I ask with a chuckle. "That was…wow."

His eyes brighten. "Wow, huh?"

"Yes, definitely wow. I'm sure my muscles will be sore tomorrow from using them, but that's okay. Reece and I scheduled some time in the spa tomorrow afternoon together, so feel free to use my muscles anyway you choose."

A wolfish grin spreads across his face. "Good to know. There're a few other positions we can try tonight," he boasts with a wink before slipping off to the restroom.

I walk over to the closet, retrieve the satin robe hanging on the hook, and slip it on. Just as I tie the knot in front, the bathroom door opens and reveals a naked Decker. Seriously, this man is drool worthy. He's the type of man they write about in romance novels. His body is perfection, all hard muscle and smooth skin. There's a matting of dark hair across his chest and a strip running down from his belly button. And don't get me started on the V. No man I've dated had anything close to the definition and deliciousness that sharp angle of his hips make. It's like a yellow flag waving, an arrow pointing down to the most impressive and talented cock I've ever had the privilege of seeing firsthand.

"Stop it or we'll never order dinner."

I look up from Decker's growing erection to meet his humor-filled eyes. "What?" I ask innocently.

He growls as he reaches for me, pulling me into his arms. "You're trouble."

Chuckling, I wrap my arms around his neck as he kisses my lips. "Trouble, sure. Hungry, mostly."

"Well, come on then. Let's order some lobster ravioli," he says, grabbing his shorts off the floor and slipping them on. My mouth waters and I couldn't hide the grin on my face if I tried.

He walks toward the nightstand where the room phone is located, and I swat his rear as he passes by. "Don't forget the dessert."

"You are practically glowing," Reece gushes the moment I step inside the spa for our joint afternoon girls' time on Tuesday afternoon.

"I don't know about that," I insist, trying to hide the blush from the resort employees standing at the counter, ready to escort us back for our treatments. Especially if everyone who works here already knows about Decker and me, they'll definitely put two and two together when it comes to the reason for my blushing glow.

Reece grins. "I do. It's from good sex."

The two women behind the counter both giggle, doing their best to cover the sound with a cough. Ignoring my new friend, I turn and say, "Adeline Montgomery. I have an appointment for a massage and facial."

"Of course, Miss Montgomery. Your massage therapist is Joss. She's ready for you," the lady with the name Gwyneth says.

"Perfect."

"Would you ladies still like the couples massage on the private balcony?"

I glance over at Reece, who's clearly not done asking all her inappropriate questions if the smirk on her face is any indication. With a sigh, I reply, "I suppose."

Reece smiles widely. "Good. The pictures of that room are breathtaking," she replies, moving to follow behind Gwyneth down the long hallway.

"Are you ladies okay using the stairs? We do have an elevator available," Gwyneth states, but I wave off her concern.

"Stairs are fine."

After going up one flight, we arrive on the second floor of the spa. Through a doorway, we're led to a beautiful area with floor-to-ceiling windows that slide open, giving the most breathtaking view of the ocean. Two entire walls are open, the warm ocean breeze kissing our skin.

"There are changing rooms there," Gwyneth announces, pointing to the closed doors. "You're welcome to wear whatever you're comfortable wearing, but we recommend stripping down to your underwear. Bras off, preferably. There's a robe hanging on the door.

You can slip that on, and your therapist will assist you in getting beneath the bedding without giving anyone a peep show."

"Thank you," I tell the woman, who nods in return as she closes the door behind her when she exits.

"This place is incredible. Well worth taking a week of vacation to join hubby on the trip," Reece states as she heads for one of the small changing rooms.

"Where is home?" I ask as I enter my own changing room, realizing we've never discussed that.

"A small town just south of Louisville, Kentucky. There's like two thousand people and three thousand horses there. I love it," she replies through the open door with a laugh.

"Do you have horses?" I ask, slipping my sundress off and hanging it on one of the available hooks.

"We have five. Royal is my favorite mare. She's simply beautiful," Reece announces, stepping out of the room in her robe. When I remove my strapless bra and place it on the stool, I don my own robe and join her in the large room. "How about you? Where are you from?"

"Charleston."

"Oh, I've been there! They have a golf course there my husband has played at."

"A few courses, yes, and a large country club."

She nods. "I'm certain it was the country club, because my husband said something about it costing more than his annual salary to play there, and he makes damn good money in investments, so it must be for the elite."

I swallow hard, trying to decide if I want to share the fact my family's name is on that particular country club or not. I'm not hiding that detail, however it's not something I usually boast about. The only people who care about your family money are people who have it. Otherwise, you're just a bragger, and no one likes a bragger.

Fortunately, the decision is taken out of my hands when Reece quickly continues. "Anyway, we take at least one big vacation a year, and always make sure there's a golf course nearby. Plus, he does dude trips with some friends once or twice a year, but I rarely go on those, unless we're on break from school. If I am, then I'll go and just hang at the hotel or resort while he does his thing. Only one of the other three guys is still married, and his wife never comes. She hates golf more than I do, and that's saying something. Plus, they have four kids, and it's impossible for her to get away. The other two are divorced, and I can totally see why. One drinks like a fish and the other was cheating on his wife with her sister."

My mind is spinning, trying to keep up with Reece. When I come out of my dressing room in my robe, I ask, "What do you do at the school?"

Reece is standing beside one of the two massage beds. "Ten years as a junior high science teacher. Kids are totally whack these days. Everything has changed so much in the last decade."

A knock sounds on the door. "May we come in?"

"Yes!" Reece declares, practically bouncing up and down with excitement.

"Good afternoon, ladies. I'm Joss, and this is Ana. We'll be giving you your massages."

"Hello," I reply as the petite brunette with a hint of Hawaiian features approaches.

The woman holds up the top sheet in a way it blocks her view of me and gives me privacy to slip out of my robe and lie down. When I'm in place on the bed with my face in the ring, she covers me up with the sheet. "Are you ready to begin?" she asks.

"Yes."

Joss pulls the sheet down and begins to massage my back. I listen as Ana asks Reece a few basic questions, who promptly replies to her questions and tells her all about the last time she had a massage. Then, we lie in silence for the next hour as our backs, legs, arms, shoulders, and necks are given a deep rubdown. The entire treatment is relaxing from the hibiscus scents to the soothing sounds of the waves and the warm ocean breeze. Even the sounds of people playing in the surf outside the resort add to the ambience.

As our massages come to an end, Joss says, "Your facials are next, but first, we'll go to the steam room. The steam helps open your pores."

"Sounds awesome," Reece says, sitting up and reaching for the robe. I do the same, and the moment it's tied around my waist, we're led to a small steam room.

Ana hands us each a small bottle of cold water and says, "Ten minutes, and we'll be ready for the next phase of your spa experience."

"This place is stunning," Reece says, taking a seat in the steam room. "Seriously, one of the top five resorts and spas I've visited."

"Agreed," I tell her, taking a welcomed sip of my cold water. "Though, I once visited this place that was in a tiki hut on the ocean. It was completely private and probably the most exclusive, world class resort I've ever been to. Oprah was there."

Reece's eyes brighten. "Really? Where was that?"

"St. Lucia," I reply, picking at invisible lint on my robe.

"I've never been. Three years ago, we went to Hawaii for our anniversary. Honua Kai was where we stayed. It was *breathtaking*," she practically sings.

I nod, having been there too. With Mother, of course. Any exclusive high-end resort where they wait on you hand and foot is always right up her alley.

"Okay, so enough about that," she says, taking a hearty drink. "Tell me about last night. I take it your dinner went...well." She grins widely.

Clearing my throat, memories of last night parade through my mind. Not only jumping him the moment he knocked on the door and the chair sex that followed, but also the strawberries and whipped cream dessert later in the evening.

"Ohhhhhhh, tell me! I want to know why you just got this dreamy look on your face and licked your lips."

"Do I have to?" I ask with a chuckle.

Her pretty face takes on a pained look. "What? You don't want to share?"

"Ummm," I start, making her laugh hard.

"Okay, fine. Don't give up the dirty deets of what you do with the sexy bartender. You're stingy, you know that?"

I can't help but giggle at her antics. "We've known each other less than a week," I reason.

Reece shrugs. "Yeah, you're probably right, but I don't have a lot of girlfriends, so I tend to overshare with perfectly good strangers," she says, flashing me a wide grin.

My heart jumps in my chest. "I don't have a lot of girlfriends either. In fact, I really only have one."

"The woman who was supposed to get married this past weekend," she derives, obviously remembering what I told her about why I was at the resort for the week.

"Yes. Audrey. We've been friends since we were younger. The women I hang out with now," I say, swallowing over the lump in my throat, "they're not really friends."

"I had a group of women I hung out with, but then over time, they started having kids and started doing things revolving around their kids. They stopped inviting me, because it was a little weird for me to tag along with them while they all talked about the stages their kids were in and I didn't have anything to add. Eventually, my phone stopped ringing."

"I'm sorry," I find myself saying, my heart hurting a little for my new friend.

She shrugs. "It's okay. I get drinks on occasion with a few co-workers, but not regularly. That's a big reason I travel with Nathanial when he goes on his golf trips. I really enjoy traveling, and you can't beat some of the resorts we've stayed at over the years. And while I love teaching and can't imagine doing anything else, I prefer to send them home at the end of the day, if you know what I mean."

I nod, understanding completely. "I get it. Kids aren't for everyone."

"No, they sure aren't. Nathanial and I are both happy just doing our thing right now. How about you? Do you want to have kids one day?"

My mind flashes to my parents, the staff who raised me, the way it felt to be brought up in a manner that led me to believe I was more of a bother than an asset. Even now, as an adult working for my father, I'm not part of the team. I'm an afterthought. I was then, and I am now. If I ever decide to bring a child into this world, it will be because I'm free to do so on my own terms and will raise that child differently, without the pressure of the Montgomery name hanging over our heads.

That's probably why I'll never have kids.

I'll never be free.

I'm firmly clutched in my father's talons with no chance of ever getting out.

I'm saved from having to answer her question when there's another knock on the door. "Ladies, if you'll follow me, we can start your facials."

"Excellent," Reece replies, standing up and moving to the exit. "Come on, Adeline. It's time to get our spa treatments on again. We're going to be glowing by the time we get to dinner this evening, and when we're done, my husband will be back from the tournament dinner, and I'll be able to show him exactly how much I appreciate him bringing me along. And you, you'll be free to continue your vacation romance with the hottie behind the bar," she adds, smiling and winking before stepping out of the steam room.

Shaking my head, I stand and follow behind her, only to find myself smiling. I *am* free to continue this *thing* between Decker and myself. A little vacation romance, if you will.

But this trip is turning into something more. I've made a new friend. Someone I enjoy spending time with and getting to know. I'm discovering all sorts of other amazing things. What I like to do, what I don't. That I have an adventurous side I've never been able to explore. That I enjoy sex a heck of a lot more than I ever thought I could or have in the past. And who knows, maybe I'll discover who I really am deep down.

That would be the greatest discovery of all.

Chapter
TWELVE

Decker

I can't help but continually watch the two women at the end of the bar, laughing and carrying on as if they've known each other for years. At a glance, you'd find it hard to believe they just met yesterday. Adeline seems relaxed and comfortable, but I'm not sure that's strictly thanks to the woman sitting beside her or if the added bonus of fruity mixed drinks is more of the culprit.

Adeline looks my way, her cheeks flushed from alcohol and whatever spa treatment she had this afternoon with Reece. They shared some of the details, but all I really understood was full body massage and a mud facial. Sounded off to wipe mud all over your face in the name of beauty, but who am I to argue? Both of them seemed refreshed and happy with the results, so I just went with it.

There are a few groups hanging around the bar this evening. Couples enjoying a late dinner or drinks, and a handful of guys at the bar who participated in the golf tournament nearby. I know that's where Reece's husband is, so I imagine he'll return to the resort soon. He's golfing with a few friends, all of whom seem to be on the prowl while staying here. In fact, I get this weird knot in the pit of my gut when I think about one of them hitting on Adeline. I have no claim to her. We have a mutually gratifying agreement for the course of her stay here, but that doesn't mean that agreement is set in stone. If she wants to entertain someone else, she's free to do so and there's not a damn thing I could do about it.

Not that I think she would. Even if she didn't insist she's never had this sort of no-strings arrangement in the past, I'd be able to tell in her demeanor. She was nervous to ask for it, which, admittedly, was part of the turn-on. I liked the fact she was a combination of confidence and shyness and her eyes seemed only interested in me. Likewise, I've only seen her since the moment she appeared at the rehearsal dinner. There's a heavy attraction there, yes, but there's other things too. A kinship, if you will, and a great deal of respect, because despite coming across as someone with money when I first met her, I know there's so much more to her.

Another bubble of laughter spills from the far end of the bar, and my feet are carrying me in their direction before I can even think about stopping. "Ladies, are we ready for another drink?" I ask, flashing Adeline a flirty grin.

"One more," Reece proclaims, her cheeks rosy and her eyes fairly glazed over.

"Ugh, I'm going to be hungover tomorrow," Adeline declares, yet still slides her empty glass my way.

"Yeah, but that's okay. Totally worth it," Reece adds. "Two more Malibu Sunsets, kind sir."

Shaking my head, I clear away their dirty glasses and retrieve two clean ones. Then, I set out to mix their drinks. It's only four simple ingredients, but it's one of our most popular mixed drink specials. Malibu coconut rum, pineapple juice, orange juice, and a splash of grenadine, garnished with a slice of orange and a maraschino cherry.

"Stop staring at his ass!" Reece bellows, making me laugh, because I already know who she's talking to.

When I return with two drinks, Adeline's cheeks are flushed from embarrassment. She reaches for the drink and starts slurping the contents through the straw. She eventually looks up and meets my gaze, so I give her a wink.

"Nathanial better hurry his ass up," Reece states, glancing at her cell phone. "There's a fine line between tipsy and drunk, and I'm teetering a little too close to the line." She sets her glass down on the coaster and leans in, holding my gaze. "Tipsy is always good, right, Decker? I mean, you get too drunk, and you're liable to stick things in the wrong hole, and unless you're into butt stuff, that's never a good thing."

I bark out a laugh, while Adeline looks like she wants the floor to open up and swallow her whole.

"Adeline, are you tipsy or drunk? I don't want you getting holes mixed up later tonight when you two get back to your room," she insists, spinning a little too quickly on her stool and swaying.

"Not drunk enough for this conversation," Adeline mumbles, greedily sucking more mixed drink from her glass.

"No? Too early for the butt stuff talk, huh? Fine. How about you, Deck? You wanna talk about butt stuff with me?"

"I see my wife is on the verge of being overserved again."

I glance up and find a tall man approaching Reece with a warm grin on his face and a lot of love reflecting in his eyes.

"'Bout time! I was about to go up to the room and start without you," Reece states loudly, drawing the attention of the small group of guys just down the bar.

The man I've been told is Nathanial chuckles at his wife before bending down and placing a kiss on her forehead. He leans in and whispers in her ear, making the tips of her ears turn dark red. I'm a little grateful not to be privy to their conversation, because something tells me it's on the dirty side.

Finally, Nathanial stands back up, wrapping his arm around Reece's back, and turns his attention to Adeline. "You must be Reece's new friend, Adeline. I've heard a lot about you."

"I am," she says, extending her hand to shake. "I've heard a lot about you as well."

He laughs lightly as he shakes her hand. "I'm sure you have. My wife is the queen of oversharing."

"We were just talking about butt stuff," she states, and I swear the guys a few chairs over all lean closer.

Nathanial smiles and shakes his head. "I don't think I want to know."

"Oh, you know!" she argues, sipping her drink.

"That was an accident," he insists, kissing her cheek.

"Yeah, I bet it was." Then she turns her attention to me. "How does that happen? Is it really an accident?"

Holding up my hands in surrender, I take a step back. "I'm just serving the drinks."

"And sleeping with my friend, Adeline," Reece counters, narrowing her eyes in my direction.

Adeline chokes on the liquid she was trying to swallow, sputtering into her hand and doing her best to not draw attention.

"Butt stuff is usually a private affair, my love. Perhaps you should quit asking the bartender about it," Nathanial states, taking a small sip from his wife's glass.

"Would you like a drink, sir?" I ask.

"No, thank you. I've had plenty for the evening." He glances over at his wife. "Just enough to be tipsy. No accidental butt stuff tonight," he adds, winking at his wife.

"Whoop!" Reece hollers, spinning on her seat and slowly standing up. Nathanial is right there, offering his arm for support, and making sure she doesn't accidentally stumble. "All right, big guy. Let's head back to our room. These two have been giving off fuck-me vibes all night, so I'm sure she's staying put. Are you staying put, Adeline?"

Poor Adeline looks horrified to be put on the spot and can't seem to get her mouth to work.

Reece tsks and leans into her husband. "She's staying." Then, because this woman apparently has no filter, she turns to the guys at the bar and adds, "Sorry, gentlemen, but my friend, Adeline, is going home with the bartender tonight. You'll have to find someone else to ogle at."

Adeline drops her head onto her arm and groans.

"All right, I'm going to take my wife to our room so she stops embarrassing you. Adeline, it was wonderful to finally meet you."

"You as well," Adeline replies with a grin.

Reece throws her arm around Adeline's neck and squeezes. "I'm so glad I met you."

Adeline smiles in return. "Me too."

Then, Reece and Nathanial make their way through the bar to the exit and head for the elevator. Once they're out of sight, I lean in and catch a whiff of her expensive perfume. "She seems great, but definitely lacks a filter."

Adeline's eyes are bright blue, but you can see the buzzed glaze over them. "Right? But do you know what? I really like her. She's unlike anyone I've ever met, and even after knowing her a short time, she's more genuine than any of the so-called friends I have back in Charleston. Audrey excluded."

A small smile spreads across my lips. "I'm glad you're enjoying your time with her."

"She's leaving first thing Thursday morning, so we've made plans to meet at the pool again tomorrow afternoon for a bit. Nathanial's last game is tomorrow, and he's supposed to be done by three, so they're having dinner and going somewhere in the evening. She invited me along, but there's no way I would tread on their time together, and no way would I want to be a third wheel."

I reach out and run my thumb across the top of her hand, watching as a shiver sweeps through her body. "I don't blame you. I'm working again tomorrow evening, but you're welcome to come down and hang out with me."

She gives me a coy smile before wrapping her plump lips around the tip of her straw. My cock jumps in my trousers as her tongue slips out and flicks against the thin plastic. "I may do that."

Unfortunately, I'm pulled away from Adeline to serve more drinks, and by the time she's reaching the end of her concoction, I can tell she's probably had enough. "You should head up to your room and get some rest," I insist as I approach, leaning in and meeting her gaze.

"Yeah," she replies through a yawn. "You're probably right."

Then, before I can say anything, she has her keycard out of her small purse and is sliding it across the bar. "You sure you want me to stop by?" I ask quietly, making sure no one can hear me.

She looks up and grins. "I'm sure."

I nod, taking the card and slipping it into the pocket of my pants. I hate to admit it, but that's not the first time I've been given a keycard. Not the first time I'll actually use it either, but it's the first time I care enough about the person giving it to me to think about more than just getting my dick wet. My first thought is to ensure she makes it to her room safely, followed by wondering if she'll take something for her head and drink plenty of water before climbing into bed.

Both thoughts leave me reeling a bit and a touch off-kilter.

"Would you like me to escort you to your room?" I ask.

"No, I'm all right," she insists, only slightly swaying on her feet when she stands. "I'm going straight there."

I nod, wishing I had someone in the bar who could cover for me for ten minutes, but there's no one here at the moment. "I'll come up as soon as I'm off work."

She smiles the softest, most beautiful smile I've ever seen, and my heart does this weird lurch in my chest. "Okay. See you soon, Decker."

I nod, my throat suddenly too tight to speak.

I watch her go, as do the other guys in the room, and when I'm certain she's made it safely to the elevator, I turn my attention back to work. I only have two more hours to go, and then I can go check on her myself. Maybe then I should head home for the night. I haven't slept in my own bed since I met Adeline, spending as much time as possible with her.

But we're also on borrowed time. She's leaving this weekend, which means I only have a few more days with her, and frankly, I'm not ready to give her up yet. I'm enjoying spending time with her too much, and I'm not just referring to the great sex. It's the whole package I'm attracted to when it comes to her.

Yeah, maybe a little distance will be a good thing.

I slip the keycard into the slot and enter her room. It's completely quiet, the shades over the sliding glass door drawn. There's a soft glow from a bedside lamp on the wall that illuminates the woman lying on the bed. She's sleeping soundly in the middle of the bed, not so much as stirring at the sound of me entering her room, but what really grabs my attention is the satin shorts and tank top set she's wearing. It's a soft pink color that looks remarkable against her tanned skin.

My mouth waters.

She moves, her long leg slipping all the way out from under the sheet, as she burrows deeper into her pillow. The softest, sweetest sigh slips from her lips as she mutters, "Decker."

I had every intention of coming up here, dropping off the keycard, and writing a note about seeing her tomorrow. A little distance is probably a good thing every now and again, considering, besides me working, we've spent almost every minute together since we both settled on this mutual agreement.

But now?

Hearing her whisper my name in the dark of night has me moving in her direction, toeing off my dress shoes without so much as bending over to untie them. I loosen the necktie and release all the small buttons on my dress shirt, tossing them both over the small table in the corner. Then, I unfasten my pants and let them drop to the floor. This is the point I'd usually grab a condom or two, but all I want to do is hold her in my arms.

Weird, right?

I've never really been what some might consider a manwhore. Yes, I've casually dated women. Yes, I've had one-night stands, probably more times than most men. I've always made my position known to every woman before taking them to bed, making sure they understood the score.

But with Adeline, it's not just about the sex.

The proof is in the fact I'm about to crawl into bed beside her and can't wait to hold her in my arms as I drift off to sleep.

I should definitely be worried about this startling revelation, but it's not as scary as I expected it to be. No, I'm not in love with her, but I do care about her. More than I ever expected I could care about someone I just met. In such a short amount of time, she has burrowed herself beneath my skin, and I have no idea what to do about it.

Spotting a bottle of water beside the bed, I swap it out for a full one and retrieve a Tylenol from the small travel bottle I saw in her bathroom. In fact, she's well prepared for just about anything. She has Band-Aids, antibacterial ointment and wipes, bug bite cream, and something for allergies.

Smiling, I slip one Tylenol from the container and return to the bedroom. I place the pill and the fresh water on the nightstand before sliding onto the mattress behind her. My cock is hard, especially after seeing her amazing ass in the tiny little satin shorts, but I ignore it. Adeline had a lot to drink tonight, and getting inside her is the last thing I'm worried about. Making sure she's taken care of comes first.

The moment I press my naked body against hers, she spins around to face me. Her right arm flings over my side and her face nuzzles into my neck. She doesn't wake, just sighs contently and relaxes in my arms.

I lie here in silence, one arm slipped beneath her neck and the other over her hip, and just breathe her in. My nose is in her hair, inhaling her sweet shampoo mixed with a unique scent that's purely Adeline. It's intoxicating, really, as is the feel of her smooth skin against mine.

I'm not sure how long I lie here and just hold her, listening to the sounds of her slowly breathing in and out, but eventually my eyes start to grow heavy. There's an additional weight on my chest as I realize our short time together is already half over. In a few days, she'll be leaving, heading home to South Carolina, and I'll be left here.

Alone.

That thought doesn't quite hold the same appeal as it once had.

Maybe it'll be time for me to move on. I've been in Florida for nine months now. Perhaps I can start to plan my next adventure, see where the roads take me. Hell, maybe they'll take me toward Charleston.

No, don't go there.

There's no point in thinking about anything past this week where Adeline is concerned. We're two totally different people, despite having a great time together. The life she leads is the one I left behind without so much as a glance back. It's best to keep my focus moving forward.

Maybe I'll check out Arizona next. Between the national parks and the ghost towns, I'm sure I'll be surrounded by beauty at every turn.

Just like Adeline.

Beauty.

At every turn.

Chapter THIRTEEN

Adeline

Two warm, soft lips press against my spine, sending shivers of desire sweeping through my body. "What time is it?" I whisper, my throat dry and my head feeling like someone's playing the bongo drums inside of it.

"Just before eight. I need to go."

I turn to face Decker. He's dressed, wearing the same dress shirt and slacks he had on at work last night. His tie is stuffed in his pants pocket. "Hot date?" I quip, smiling at my own joke. Mostly because I've never been comfortable enough around a man to joke like this.

"Why, yes, actually. I promised Marian I'd mow her lawn this morning and help her spread some mulch around a few trees before it gets too hot."

"Oh," I reply, throwing the sheet off me and sitting up. "You're going to help Marian?"

He nods, reaching out and swiping an erratic hair off my forehead and cheek. "This is a cute look for you."

I swipe at his hand and run my own hand over my head. I can feel my hair sticking up everywhere, no doubt thanks to the rough night of sleep I had at the expense of too many fruity Malibu Sunset drinks. "I feel like I got hit by a small bus."

His low chuckle goes straight to the apex of my legs. "A small bus?"

"You know, one of those shorter, smaller ones. Not a big bus. I don't feel like death, just a little maimed."

"Alcohol will do that to you," he quips. "What time do you meet Reece later?"

"We're meeting at the tiki bar by the pool around eleven thirty and then just hanging out for a bit until her husband finishes the tournament," I reply, adjusting the spaghetti strap on my right shoulder after it slips down.

He's staring at my hand, his eyes sweeping across my skin like a gentle embrace. "Wanna go with me?"

"With you?" My voice sounds deep and husky, my nipples pebble against the satin material of my tank top.

Decker notices, of course. His eyes zero in on my chest, devouring every inch of me with laser-sharp focus. "Fuck," he mutters, running his hand down his face. "I want to strip you naked and have my wicked way with you."

"I like the sound of that," I insist.

He chuckles and shakes his head. "Later, Addi. I promised Marian I'd help her, and if I don't get off this bed right this second, I won't be leaving this room anytime soon."

I lower my shoulder, letting the single strap fall once more. "I don't see a problem with that."

Decker leans forward and kisses me hard on the lips. "I need to go meet Marian," he says without deepening the kiss and standing up to put distance between us.

"Do you think you'll be done by eleven thirty?"

Hands on his hips, he nods. "Should be. It usually takes me an hour or so to mow, and then maybe thirty minutes to spread her mulch."

Suddenly feeling a bit nervous, I fumble with my hands in my lap. "Then I'd love to go with you. I'd enjoy sitting with Marian and visiting while you mow."

He smiles. "I think she'd enjoy that. How quickly can you be ready?"

I jump up, already moving toward the bathroom. "I need to run through the shower and brush my teeth, so give me twenty minutes?" The moment he nods, I shut the door and get to work. I've never gone out in public the way I'm about to, without full makeup or with wet hair, but do you know what? I don't care. I'm excited to hang out with Decker's elderly neighbor lady for a while, and if someone somehow looks down on me because I'm not completely one-hundred-percent photograph ready, then so be it.

Screw them.

I blush a little bit at that thought. My mother would have a field day with my use of that word.

My shower is short and sweet, and before I know it, I'm standing in front of the foggy mirror in a towel and getting ready. I brush my teeth, floss, and use mouthwash, and then switch to my morning facial routine. I still cleanse and moisturize, but instead of all the normal makeup, I stick with a little mascara. My face is still glowing, thanks to yesterday's facial treatment mixed with the sun, but it has a more natural look to it, and if I'm being honest, I like it.

A lot.

After brushing out my hair, I opt to leave it down, loose and wet, and slip on the sundress I brought into the bathroom. I forgo panties— of course, blushing the entire time—as well as a bra. Thanks to my small breasts, it's not always necessary with the right material. I try not to think about the fact I'm not wearing anything beneath my dress, but it's difficult. Especially when my mind conjures up images of Decker discovering that tidbit of information later this evening.

Finally, I give myself a quick once-over and open the door. Decker is out on the balcony, watching the water. He must hear me, because he turns around, his eyes immediately dropping to take in my appearance. Does he know I'm not wearing anything beneath this dress? Do I have a sign on my forehead advertising it?

"Ready?" he asks, stepping inside and shutting the door behind him.

"Yes."

He approaches, eyes sweeping up and down my lean body with every step he takes. When he's directly in front of me, he bends slightly and places a soft, gentle kiss on my lips. "That dress is coming off later, Addi."

"Promises, promises," I tease, dancing my fingers up his dress shirt.

"I suppose I might be willing to lose my dress as long as you're willing to lose your pants."

He smirks and reaches for my hand, tucking it firmly inside his. "That seems to be a regular occurrence with you, Addi. I'm always willing to lose my pants when you're around."

I grab my clutch, and hand in hand, we exit the room. Once we approach the elevator, we run into two women in uniforms, pulling cleaning carts. They both glance up and do a double take when their eyes land on Decker. Expecting him to drop my hand, I'm surprised when he doesn't. He nods at the two women, offers a happy "Good morning" greeting, and then escorts me onto the elevator when the door opens.

"You okay?" he asks when we're alone and descending.

"Yes. Are you? They're probably going to start talking about seeing us together."

Decker shrugs, bringing my hand to his mouth and kissing my knuckles. "Don't care. Let them."

Those two simple words.

Let them.

When have I ever just let the people around me talk, without caring what they're saying? Never. I've always been worried about what others think of me or see when they look my way. It was engrained in my soul from birth to care. But listening to Decker blow off the potential gossip involving us is…refreshing. I *so* want to do the exact same thing and let it go.

Let them.

Let them talk, let them come to their own conclusions, let them believe what they want to believe.

Let them.

"You okay?"

His question pulls me from my own head, and I offer a small smile. "Yes," I answer truthfully.

"Good." The door chimes and opens into the lobby. "Let's go see Marian. If you're lucky, she baked peach cinnamon rolls." My stomach chooses that moment to growl, making him laugh. "Come on," he adds, guiding me from the elevator and down the back hallway toward the rear exit. We pass a handful of employees as we go, but no one says anything to us, even though you can see their surprise and questions in their eyes as we pass.

We settle inside his car and are heading toward his small rental within a few minutes. I roll down the window and let the morning breeze wash over me. My hair flies everywhere, but I don't care. I smile anyway, wishing I could somehow save this feeling. Maybe bottle it up, so I can pull it out and feel it again sometime.

Hair wild, barely any makeup, and happier than I think I've ever been in my entire life.

Decker doesn't say a word, just reaches over and takes my hand. We're both content to just sit here, enjoying the ride and the silence. It's so comfortable, it's as if we've been doing this very mundane task together for much longer than we have.

He pulls into his small driveway and parks. I spot movement almost instantly and find Marian working in one of her flower beds. I don't wait for him to come around and open my door. I have it open and am climbing out within seconds, eager to spend a little time with the older woman.

"Good morning, Marian," I say as we approach.

She clearly heard our arrival and is waiting for us, a happy smile spreading across her face. "I was hoping I'd get to see you again, Adeline. I'm so glad you're here."

I'm immediately engulfed in a hug. "I thought I'd come keep you company while Decker mows your lawn."

She nods in delight. "That's a wonderful idea! I made some of my peach cinnamon rolls. They're fresh from the oven and still warm," she says, taking my arm and leading me to the table and chairs beneath the pergola.

"Those are my favorite," Decker says as he places a gentle kiss on Marian's cheek.

"I'm aware. I'll save two for you for later."

He seems a bit surprised by her comment. "What? I don't get one now? But…they're still warm," he mumbles, clearly not happy he's being told he has to work first before he gets one of the rolls.

Marian laughs. "Oh, stop being a whiner. Yes, you can have one now, and the other afterward." She looks my way. "I just love riling him up."

I chuckle as Decker narrows his eyes at the older woman he clearly adores. "That wasn't nice. I was about to accidentally scalp a strip right down the middle of your yard," he says, the humor dancing in his eyes as he teases Marian.

She gasps. "You wouldn't dare!"

Decker shrugs and reaches for a cinnamon roll. "Not anymore, but let that be a lesson to you, missy."

She laughs and shakes her head. "You know I would never keep you from one of my treats, Decker. I make them just for you anyway."

"Well, in that case, I get all these, right?"

Marian is already shaking her head. "You do not, sir. My new friend, Adeline, gets as many as she'd like."

Decker sighs dramatically. "Fine. I'm going to change my clothes and get the yard mowed so we can spread the mulch. I'm probably going to trim the bushes and the big tree too. I noticed one of the branches is hanging a little low, and I don't want you to walk into it."

She grins adoringly at the man who's stuffing his face with half a cinnamon roll. "You're too good to me, Decker."

He swallows his mouthful and bends down to kiss her cheek. "I could say the same about you, Marian. Enjoy your visit. I'll be done in just a bit." Then he's off to change his clothes and get to work.

"Come on, Adeline, have a seat in that chair there," she says, pointing to the far one that faces the house. "You'll have the best view when he's working," she adds with a wink.

I can't help but giggle. "Marian."

"What?" she asks innocently. "I'm old but not dead. He has a great body, especially when he takes his shirt off." She winks and settles into the chair right beside me, facing the large backyard that will require Decker's mowing.

I help pour two glasses of lemonade, while Marian places a cinnamon roll onto two small plates. "Decker was hoping you'd make these," I tell her as I glance around for a fork.

"I'm sure he was. He loves them." As if understanding what I'm searching for, she lifts her gooey roll up and says, "Part of the joy of eating these is using your hands." Then, she takes a hearty bite, smearing frosting and peaches on her lips.

I glance down at the delicious pastry, realizing I've probably never eaten with my hands before. I grab the roll and bring it to my lips, taking a smaller bite, which is no less messy, by the way. "Oh my God," I mutter, mouth full of the mouthwatering pastry.

"Right?" she asks, before taking another bite of her own. "Eat up, and then we'll chat."

When we've both polished off one of her infamous rolls, I find myself leaning back in the comfortable chair, despite the nagging in the back of my mind telling me to sit up straight. *A lady always has good posture.*

"Now that those are out of the way, tell me about you. Where are you from?"

"Charleston," I state, taking a small sip of my lemonade.

"Pretty area, from what I hear."

"It is," I confirm.

"And what do you do there?"

My throat gets thick for some reason, but I'm able to answer her anyway. "I'm an attorney."

"An attorney? Wow, that's exciting," she boasts.

I shrug my shoulders and reach for the glass of lemonade once again, just to give my hand something to do. "It is, I suppose," I say before I can stop the words.

Her head cocks to the side a touch. "You don't like it?"

I open my mouth to insist I do, but that's not what comes out. "It's just a bit…different than I thought it'd be."

"How so?"

"Well, I thought I'd actually be doing attorney work," I find myself saying, thinking back on the work I've done at the firm since graduating law school and passing my bar exam. "Instead, I seem to be the one doing all the grunt work behind the scenes. Don't get me wrong, I know I need to pay my dues, but I'm certain that's not what this is. I graduated with another associate, and he's already seeing courtroom time. I have yet to set foot inside one."

"Well, that doesn't seem right," she insists.

"No, it doesn't. Especially since I work twice as hard as Ethan Hatherley." I should stop talking, but I find the words pouring from my mouth now that I've started and can't seem to zip my lips. "We started off in the same small office area. I've seen what he calls work. He passes off any real research onto me or one of the paralegals, is on his phone nonstop all day, and takes two-hour lunches. Yet, when a big case came up for counsel assignment this past week, one I had been doing all the research and legwork on, they assigned him the case." I take a deep breath. "My father was the partner who assigned it to him."

"That doesn't seem right at all, dear."

I shake my head. "It's not. My father doesn't want me to succeed," I confess, dropping my gaze to the delicate ivory lace tablecloth.

"Well, that's hogwash!" Marian bellows, dismayed on my behalf.

A smile spreads across my lips. "It is."

"I'm tempted to have a chat with that man," Marian states, clearly agitated on my behalf.

"I appreciate it, but that's not necessary."

"Well, take it from me and my eighty-two years of life experience. Don't let him or any man walk all over you. Stand your ground, Adeline. You only get one shot at living your life, so do it on your terms, not someone else's."

A lump the size of Texas is firmly lodged in my throat, making it hard to breathe. Add in the sudden onslaught of moisture in my eyes, and I can barely see. I'm not much of a crier—I've been trained to always conceal my emotions—but listening to Marian give me sound advice has me on the verge of waterworks.

Blinking rapidly, I look up to see Decker appear on the side of the house, pushing a mower. His shirt is off, hanging from his back pocket, with muscles and tattoos all on display. He's wearing a ball cap pulled down low to keep the sun out of his eyes, light-colored, well-worn blue jeans, and athletic shoes. His gait is powerful, confident, and sexy as hell. It's impossible not to stare.

"See what I mean? He's quite nice to look at," Marian announces, breaking through the fog in my brain as she sips her lemonade.

I bark out a laugh, covering my mouth with my hand, but realizing quickly how little I actually care that I might appear unladylike. Reaching for my own glass, I take a small sip before confirming, "Yes, Marian, he is. He's quite nice to look at indeed."

Chapter

FOURTEEN

Decker

The water is hot but feels soothing against my heated skin. Thankfully, Marian's yard is well shaded, and the amount of time I'm in direct sun is fairly minimal. That's a big part of the reason why I insist on doing her yardwork in the mornings, before the heat of the day gets too intense, but I've also resorted to early evenings a time or two, depending on my schedule.

I couldn't help but steal glimpses of Adeline and Marian as they visited while I worked. They seemed to be enjoying themselves, laughing and having fun throughout the morning, and that made me feel good. Not only because I'm sure the visit did Marian some good, but also Adeline. There are times where I sense she's lonely in her life, and it was all but confirmed when she told me about her parents and her lack of real friends back in Charleston. If spending a little time with Marian brings that smile to her gorgeous face, then I'll happily drive her over here for a visit every chance I get.

Unfortunately, I don't see that happening. It's Wednesday, and as far as I know, Adeline's leaving Saturday to go home. I'm not sure how she's going home yet, considering she doesn't have a car, but she says she'll figure that out when the time comes.

We have plenty of time for me to shower before I promised to have her back at the resort for her planned lunch with Reece. Then, I think I'll come back and take a nap. Since I don't work until four, there's no need for me to hang around the resort. Maybe I'll run and pick up some groceries, so my fridge has a little more substance in it. Not that I plan to be here for many meals over the next few days, but once Adeline returns to South Carolina, I'll find myself with plenty of time on my hands again.

That thought makes my stomach churn.

Pushing it from my mind, I reach for the shampoo and squirt a glob in the palm of my hand. Just as I'm about to lather my hair, the shower curtain is pulled back, exposing a very naked Adeline. I don't say a word as she steps into the tub and closes the curtain before turning and facing me.

The water spray is coating her amazing body, and her nipples are hard and making my mouth water. "I thought you already took a shower today," I state, my eyes lazily sliding down her torso to her pussy.

"Yes, I did, but it was...warm out there. The view was so spectacular, it kept getting me all hot and bothered."

My eyes widen, mostly because I never imagined those words would fall out of her pretty little mouth. "Yeah? What view was that?" I ask, letting the shampoo wash from my hands as I reach for her.

"The shirtless lawn boy."

I snort a laugh. "Hardly a boy, Addi. All man." I run my hand down her back, cupping the globe of her perfect ass.

She arches her back, leaning forward and pressing her tits to my chest. With her eyes locked on mine, she reaches for my hard cock and gives it a gentle squeeze. "Yes, it seems you are correct. All man."

A growl erupts from my throat as I slam my mouth against hers, coaxing her lips apart and delving in deep. She wraps one arm around my neck, while slowly stroking me from root to tip. Then, before I can say anything else, she's dropping to her knees in front of me and my mind goes completely blank.

Water hits Adeline in the head, so I quickly turn the nozzle to miss her face. She adjusts her position and draws the tip of my dick to her mouth, circling it with her tongue. Then, she slowly wraps her lips around my cock and practically swallows it.

My eyes cross as I reach to the side with my hand, using the wall of the shower as leverage. I inhale a deep breath as her lips glide over my cock, applying just enough suction to ensure I'm unable to process a single thought. All I can do is stand here and feel.

Gazing down, I get lost in her movement, in the euphoria she creates. She twists her hand slightly and pulls me in deeper with her mouth. I should be embarrassed by how quickly I'm going to come, but I can't seem to find the ability to worry about it. All I can do is focus on the pleasure, and fuck, there's so much of it.

"Going to come," I mutter through gritted teeth. My intention is to give her advance warning, because I'm not going to assume she's a woman who likes to swallow.

"Good," she whispers, licking the underside of my cock and sending fire racing up my spine.

Then, she goes in for the kill. Adeline wraps her lips around me once more and sucks hard, twisting her hand as she moves and sending me straight into orbit. My balls draw up tight as I release cum down her throat, my body convulsing and shaking as my orgasm races through me.

Finally, after what feels like several minutes, I'm able to breathe again and open my eyes. Adeline is grinning up at me, a satisfied look on her beautiful face. "Well, that was unexpected," I say, reaching down to help her stand.

"But was it…okay?"

I snort in dismay. "Okay? Darlin', it was better than okay. You fucking blew my mind," I reassure her, placing a kiss on the tip of her nose.

"Well, technically, I didn't blow your *mind*…"

A bark of laughter flies from my mouth. "No, you definitely blew something else." My mouth crashes against hers. We don't have much time before I have to take her back to the resort, but I'm certain it's just enough for me to get her off with my mouth.

"Put your hand on the wall and your foot on the side of the tub." She does as instructed, but with questions in her eyes. Then, I drop to my knees and grin. "Now, hang on, Addi. It's your turn to have your mind blown."

I pull away from the resort and head toward my house. I have a few more hours to kill before I'm due at work, and thanks to getting a jump on the yard work earlier this morning, that's all crossed off my list.

Adeline was excited to go have her final luncheon with Reece, and even though she didn't say it, I know she'll ask to keep in contact after the other couple leaves to return home. I hope they do. They might be as different as night and day, but they seem to get along well and enjoy each other's company.

As I'm driving up the coast, enjoying the sunshine, my mind jumps to my friend Todd. We communicate through calls or text somewhat often, though I haven't seen him in almost a year. I was able to pop in for a visit before I relocated to Florida and spend a couple days with him and his family. He became my sounding board once my grandfather died. He's also the only person who knows all the shit I've dealt with in regard to my father and doesn't judge me for the detoured path I chose in life, instead of the one laid in front of me.

Cueing up my phone on the dash, the call rings three times before he answers. "I was just thinking about you," he says in way of greeting.

"Yeah? Recalling how ridiculously good-looking I am and wishing you stood half the chance with the ladies?" I tease, smiling as his laughter filters through the speakers.

"Uhh, no. I'm certain I'm the better-looking friend, and Lisa would have my balls roasted if I so much as thought about trying to pick up someone else."

"Truth. She's fierce," I say, drumming my thumb on the steering wheel.

"She is, but you know there's no way in hell I'd risk hurting or losing her. I only have eyes for my wife."

"Yeah, I know that. I just love riling you up," I answer.

"So, tell me what's going on with you?"

"I'm not interrupting anything, am I?"

"Nope. Between meetings. Your timing is excellent."

"How's the family?" I inquire, but he quickly cuts me off.

"Nope, I asked you first. What's up?"

I sigh. "Can't a guy call his oldest friend to say hi?"

"Sure," Todd says, and I can practically hear him kicking back in his chair, getting comfortable. "But when you're just calling to chat, it's usually during the weekend sometime, and not the middle of the workday. So, spill."

I don't say anything for several long seconds, but ultimately decide I called him for a reason. He knows it. I know it. "I met someone."

"Ahhh, now we're getting into the nitty-gritty. Tell me about her," Todd insists, his voice holding a hint of joy.

"She's..." I pause, trying to find the right word to describe her. "Amazing. An attorney who is just as beautiful on the inside as she is on the outside."

"Brains and beauty? What the hell's she doing with you?" he quips, making me relax and laugh.

"Believe me, I wonder the same thing," I reply, pulling into a lot near a coastal shopping center and parking my car.

"So what's the problem?" he asks gently.

"She lives in Charleston."

"Ahh, I see. You like her, and she's leaving."

"Yeah," I reply, closing my eyes for a few moments and just breathing.

"Well, I hate to be the one to state the obvious here," he starts, but I interrupt him.

"Don't hold back. There's a reason I called you. I need your thoughts."

"Okay, well, here's the thing. You've known this woman, what? A few days?"

My throat gets tight and it's suddenly hard to swallow. "Since Friday, really."

"Okay, so five days. Is that long enough to truly know someone?"

His question bothers me, but only because I'd be asking the same thing if the roles were reversed. I don't fault my friend at all for where his mind is leading him, but I also don't like him questioning my feelings for Adeline.

With a deep exhale, I concede. "Yeah, you're right."

"Always," he quips with a short chuckle before clearing his throat. "On the other hand, I've never seen you like this, my friend. For you to even be mentioning her to me tells me more than you probably realize."

"Like what?"

"Well, how about the fact you've not talked about one woman since you left Norfolk when you were twenty-three."

"I've dated."

"I'm certain you have, but the fact she's worth mentioning to me and has your mind all twisted is saying something."

"I guess," I mutter, feeling a headache coming on.

"You've lived in how many places over the last seven years?"

"I don't know."

"Close to a dozen?"

"Probably," I reply, doing quick math and realizing he's fairly close.

"And in those twelve or so cities, you've not so much as mentioned one single woman to me. Why do you think that is?"

I open my mouth to reply, but nothing comes out.

"I'll tell you why," he continues, "because you're falling for this woman. Hard and fast and it scares the shit out of you."

"I care about her," I confess, even though it's not new information to me.

"Of course you do, which is why you're upset. She's leaving soon, going home, and you don't know what to do about it."

"I can't ask her to stay," I counter. "That'd be silly."

"Probably," he agrees easily. "But what's your reason for staying in Florida?"

"Marian." That answer is easy.

"I can understand that, and it definitely adds a layer of complication to the equation, but let me ask you this. If this woman—" he pauses.

"Adeline."

"If this woman, Adeline, asks you to go to Charleston with her, would you?"

In a heartbeat.

Realizing that makes my heart stumble in my chest and my breathing shallow.

"You would, wouldn't you?" he asks softly.

"Yeah."

"Well, there's your answer. What did I tell you about Lisa when she agreed to go out with me junior year of high school?"

A smile spreads across my face as I recall the exact conversation. "You told me you were going to marry her one day."

"I knew right then and there. It was a feeling I had deep in my soul. I knew I would do whatever I could to spend the rest of my life with her," he says, the hint of a smile in his voice.

"Speaking of, how's Lisa?" I ask, happy to change the subject for a bit.

"She's perfect. She wants to have another baby."

"Do it. Literally. Do you need pointers?" I josh, poking the bear.

"Fuck off, I don't need pointers. I've managed to do this three times already," he counters, making me laugh.

"What's your holdup?" I ask. I've known Todd most of my life, and I can imagine he has an issue or two holding him back. Otherwise, she'd be pregnant already.

"We're already outnumbered, man. Three kids under seven is intense. Do we want to make it four under eight?"

"You're a great dad, Todd. If anyone can handle four kids, it's you and Lisa."

He sighs happily. "Thanks, man. Honestly, I'll probably agree. Watching my wife grow my child and bring him or her into the world is the best. There's nothing like it." He clears his throat before adding, "Speaking of dads, I saw yours a few weeks ago."

I sit up taller in my seat, my spine stiff with anxiety. "What happened?"

"He said you weren't responding to his attorney and asked if I've talked to you lately."

My throat is Sahara dry. "What did you say?"

"Told him I hadn't talked to you and wished him a nice day," he states pointedly.

Exhaling a breath I didn't realize I was holding, I reply, "I haven't spoken to his attorney directly, but mine has."

Todd sighs. "I hate that it came down to this."

"Me too," I agree, glancing around at the people milling through the shopping area. "He's pissed about the money. Thinks I should be forced to support the business."

"Such bullshit. The fact he's still focused on that shit instead of just running the company. Why try to force you into it?"

I've been wondering the same thing. "I don't know, man."

I can hear a knock through the phone, followed by a soft murmur. "Thank you, Glenda. Listen, Deck, my next appointment is here."

"I'm glad I caught you when I did. Thanks for giving me a little time," I tell him honestly.

"Always. We'll talk again soon."

"Great, and maybe I'll try to get up to Norfolk soon," I say, realizing how much I'd like to make a trip to see him.

"Lisa would be thrilled."

"And if she's not pregnant by then, I'll be able to give you some pointers," I tease, laughing when he growls through the phone line.

"Fuck off."

Chuckling, I add a quick, "Talk to you soon."

"Bye."

Then, he's gone, leaving me alone in my car with only my thoughts. It doesn't surprise me my dad would stoop so low as to inquire about my whereabouts with my oldest friend, but the truth is, he knows exactly where I am. I've never hid. He has the money and resources to find me, but once he told me to get the fuck out of his office and his life, I did just that. The only reason he's contacting me now is because of money.

Because he wants it.

I end up rolling down my window before pulling out of the lot. My car heads for the seaside highway, and I just drive. My mind is all over the place. I think back on my conversation with Todd. I smile at the thought of him and Lisa having another baby but can definitely see his worry. Four kids? That's a lot of chaos, but if anyone can handle it, it's Todd and Lisa. They were destined to be together from the beginning, and while their marriage is far from perfect, they've worked hard on it throughout the years.

It doesn't surprise me he picked up on the reason for my call. Not only did I want to hear from my friend, but I needed a bit of advice. I expected him to tell me it was too soon to be all up in my feels where Adeline is concerned. Didn't like it but expected it. What I didn't antic-ipate was him to do a one-eighty and basically point out the fact I'm falling for her.

How is that possible?

It only adds to my confusion, and even though talking to Todd didn't give me the magical answers I needed, it grounded me a bit. It helped me to know my feelings are real, even if I don't understand them.

Decisions don't have to be made today, but they will have to be soon. She's leaving Saturday, and I don't know if I have it in me to try a long-distance relationship. Yes, as he pointed out, there's nothing major holding me here, with the exception of my friendship with Marian, but even that, she knew by renting me the guesthouse, it was most likely a short-term situation.

That particular relationship only adds to the deep churning in my gut, because even though my living here has always been considered temporary, I feel a connection with the older woman. She's like an extension of the grandparents I've lost, and our friendship means a great deal to me.

With a sigh, I turn up the music and let the Florida heat wrap around me. I may not know the answers to all the questions bouncing around in my head, but one thing is certain.

Either way, I'm losing something important to me.

Chapter
FIFTEEN

Adeline

I'm a little sad as Reece and her husband leave the resort on Thursday morning. My new friend is returning home, and while we exchanged numbers and promises to keep in touch, I'm feeling a bit melancholy at her departure. In a matter of days, Reece has shown me friendship that doesn't revolve around my last name or my family legacy. In fact, she doesn't know about any of it. She reminds me a bit of Audrey, and I find myself craving the normalcy she provides.

Decker is filling in for another employee for a shift at the tiki bar by the pool, and while we haven't made plans for afterward, I think we both know I'll be heading down to enjoy a little sun by the pool this afternoon. I mean, there's no way I want to miss seeing Decker in shorts and a Hawaiian button-up, the uniform of the resort staff outside around the pool area.

Donning my own festive floral bikini, I slip on a white cover-up and grab my large bag. As I move through my room, I spot my phone in the same spot on the dresser where it's sat much of my time here. I'm still not ready to turn it on and deal with the fallout of sending that email last Saturday night. I know my father is still trying to reach me, and by now, I'm certain he's furious with me. I've ignored him for far longer than I ever have, and I know my actions will eventually come to a head.

There's only so long I can ignore him.

That's a fact.

But today isn't going to be the day I turn on the device. I walk right past it, slip my bag over my shoulder, and exit my room. There's a sexy man down at the bar I long to see, even though I just saw him a few hours ago.

As I step off the elevator on the ground floor, my eyes are drawn to the small boutique. Instead of heading straight for the pool area, I walk to the shop and open the door. I'm instantly drawn to the gorgeous garments on display, noting the vivid colors and cool textiles. I've made several purchases down here in the last few days, considering I wasn't planning to stay an additional week, and with each visit, I find something new to appreciate.

Today, there's a small display of resort logo polos, T-shirts, and beach accessories to check out as you first walk in. I pick up a T-shirt in a subtle pink color and run my hand over the cotton. I don't think I've ever felt a shirt this soft, not that I own many T-shirts. In fact, I have approximately two and never wear them.

I walk over to where the dresses are displayed next. There are a variety of styles and colors. Everything from casual sundresses—like the ones I've been buying—to more formal dinner options for a night out. Little black dresses to red sparkly numbers. Even some gorgeous white ones that could easily pass for the perfect beach wedding.

"Oh, hello, Miss Montgomery."

I turn and smile at Hazel, the woman who runs the boutique. "Hazel, lovely to see you again."

The perfectly put together woman offers me a warm smile. "You know, we received a shipment in this morning, and one of the pieces just screamed your name."

"Really?" I ask, my mind spinning at all the possibilities.

"Yes, would you care to see it?"

"Of course!" I exclaim eagerly, approaching the counter as she walks through a closed door.

When the door opens, I'm instantly drawn to the vibrant colors. Coral flowers with a navy background that's both eye-catching and complementary. "It's not the usual dress you've purchased from us recently, but it just screamed your name when I saw it," she informs me, placing the outfit on the counter.

Except, it's not a dress.

It's a two-piece pants set.

"The top has a thick halter-style strap that ties at the neck. It should hit just above the belly button, and the bottom has an elastic band around the waist and gentle, flowy material all the way down to the ankles. Depending on what shoes you wear, it can be dressed up with heels or down a bit with sandals. Pair it with a camel-colored straw hat and those cute little wedge sandals you have, and it would make the most beautiful summer ensemble," she states confidently as I finger the soft material.

"I'll take it," I state, catching her off guard.

"Would you care to try it on?"

Hazel is well aware I prefer to try on clothes before I purchase them. With my tall five-ten stature, it's a requirement. So many cute pieces are designed with the average height woman in mind. That's a big reason why I generally stick to dresses or clothes specifically labeled for tall women. "I should, but I don't think I'm going to."

"Well, if you put it on and it doesn't suit your needs, you're welcome to bring it back for store credit," she tells me, taking the outfit and slipping it inside one of her shopping bags.

I glance over my shoulder and head for the display of resort logo items. I grab the soft pink colored T-shirt in a size large, knowing it will be big on me. But I envision sleeping in the shirt, and for that, it'll need to be a bigger size.

Before I return to the counter, I spot a selection of straw hats. One is big and floppy and the perfect camel color to offset the dress. It also has a string of beads around it that gives it the perfect Boho feel. I slip it on my head to ensure it fits and return to the counter.

"Oh, lovely choice," Hazel agrees, nodding her approval. "I'm going to display this outfit later this weekend and I'll be sure to add a similar hat."

"Patrons will love it," I assure her, placing my additional purchases on the counter. "If you add those adorable straw sandals with the navy-blue flowers on the top, I think they'd really bring the entire outfit together."

Hazel is pleased with my suggestion and smiles widely. "Perfect!

Thank you for the tip." She leans in a bit, and adds, "I couldn't interest you in a pair of those sandals, can I?" She winks, making me laugh.

"Not today. I'm going to wear those straw wedges you were talking about, but if I change my mind, I know where to find you."

She beams at me, ringing up the T-shirt and hat, and slipping them inside the large bag. "Charged to your room?"

"Yes, please."

She enters a few things onto her computer screen. "Would you like this bag sent to your room?"

"That would be perfect," I reply, feeling lighter and happier. Not because shopping particularly makes me happy, but I truly enjoy putting together outfits and finding styles to fit and complement all body types.

It's one of my secret passions in life.

"Enjoy the afternoon, Miss Montgomery," Hazel states, taking my bag and placing it on the counter behind her.

"You as well, Hazel."

With a smile on my face, I head for the pool area.

It's a bit busier than it has been the last few days, with more couples and even a few small families checking in for what I assume is a long weekend. My eyes instantly find the bartender, who is smiling at two women sitting in front of him. A pang of jealousy startles me, but I quickly squash it down. I have no business being jealous of those two women. I might be sleeping with Decker, but I have no claim to him. In a matter of forty-eight hours, I'll be returning to South Carolina, our time together growing more distant with each mile that separates us.

He glances over and smiles.

I recognize his smile immediately. His eyes crinkle around the edges and his jaw relaxes a touch, and it's nothing like the one he was just giving the two women before him. This one is real, and dare I say, all for me?

I confidently walk in his direction, adding a little extra sway to my hips as I move. His eyes track me every step of the way as I sashay past the two women in barely-there bikinis and take a seat at the far end of the bar. He's already heading toward me, his eyes roaming over my body like a gentle caress.

"Well, good afternoon, Adeline," he says, dropping a coaster in front of me. "Can I get you a drink?"

"Yes. I'll try one of your daily specials, please."

His eyebrows draw up as he smiles widely. "Drinking already?"

I nod, placing my bag on the vacant seat beside me. "I am. It's a gorgeous day, after all, and the view is…" I let my eyes scan him from head to as far down as I can see without the view being blocked by the bar, "is spectacular."

He smiles warmly, a hint of naughty laced in those lips. "I do agree with you. You can't beat this view."

"I would like to order lunch as well," I inform him, taking a small sip of the ice water he places in front of me.

"Of course. Our special today is a mahi-mahi salad with a pineapple and mango glaze and roasted vegetables."

"Sounds delicious. I'll have that."

He nods, turning to place my order on the computer before starting my drink. I watch in rapture, mesmerized by his movements and actions. I've never paid any attention to the individuals making my drinks, but when that person is Decker, I can't stop staring.

"And what might your plans be on this beautiful day?" he asks, placing the drink on a second coaster.

"Well, I purchased a gorgeous new outfit at the boutique inside. I think I'll wear it tomorrow."

He leans forward, his big hands splayed on the bar top. "Yeah? Big plans tomorrow?"

I shrug casually, bringing the drink to my lips and taking a sip. "Wow, this is delicious. What's in it?"

"Tequila and grapefruit juice."

"That's it?" I ask, taking a second sip.

"That's it," he confirms, his eyes following my every move. "Salted rim and a grapefruit wedge garnish. All very basic, but very good."

I nod, returning it to the coaster. "Salty Dog. I like it."

He grins, turning toward the opposite end of the bar as the other employee approaches. "I'll be back."

I watch as he begins to make drinks for the other employee. Decker is good at his job, very charismatic, and is quick with a smile. He adds a few extra cherries to a pink colored drink and places it on the tray before turning to the computer and typing in the orders.

When he's finished and heads my way, I can't help but ask. "What was the last drink? The one with the extra cherries. It looked good."

He chuckles, propping his elbows on the bar and leaning toward me. "Kiddie Cocktail." He points toward the pool to the little girl with long blond hair, a pink swimsuit, and purple princess arm floaties sitting on a shaded lounge chair. "Her name is Arabella. She's on vacation with her parents and older brother, and when they first got here, she came right up to me and asked if I knew how to make a kiddie cocktail. I assured her I did, which made her smile. She told me the cherries were her favorite part before running over to meet up with her family and secure their seats. That's her second one, and I make sure to include extra cherries for her."

My heart skips a beat in my chest, rendering me speechless. This man. He's the sweetest, most caring person I think I've ever met. He puts off this dangerous, bad boy vibe, but I can see through it. He's loyal to those he cares about and is sweet to everyone he meets, including kids.

And that gets me picturing things I shouldn't. Images of Decker holding a newborn baby fill my mind. Him playing ball with a son in the backyard and walking around Marian's flower garden with a daughter on his shoulders.

"Where'd ya go there?" he asks.

Nothing gets by him.

"I was just thinking how sweet it is you give that little girl extra cherries."

He flashes me a wide grin. "Well, they're her favorite." A man appears with a tray of food, and Decker turns and takes the dish, placing it in front of me. He grabs a wrapped set of silverware from beneath the bar and places it beside my salad and takes my water glass to top it off.

"This smells fantastic," I state, unwrapping my fork.

"It tastes even better," he replies with a wink, his voice low and husky, which makes my thighs clench. He stands up straight, his attention being pulled to the opposite end of the bar. "I'll be back to check on you."

I nod and dive into my food, appreciating the sweet glaze over the delicious, flaky fish. It's served over a bed of fresh greens, topped with roasted vegetables and a fruity dressing I wouldn't normally think would work with a salad. The result is positively scrumptious, like every other meal I've had during my stay here.

As I'm approaching the end of my lunch, he returns to where I'm seated. "Sorry to leave you hanging. It got busy there for a bit," he says, referring to the dozens of drinks he's made for guests hanging around the pool.

"No problem. You are working, after all," I quip, wiping my mouth and pushing my plate away. "I'm stuffed. That was delicious."

He takes the nearly empty plate and stacks it in a plastic bin. "Can I interest you in dessert?" There's a touch of heat written in those brown eyes that makes me shiver with anticipation.

Leaning forward, I softly ask, "Depends. Are you on the menu?"

He smiles widely as he edges closer, licking his lips. "That can definitely be arranged, though I was kinda hoping *you* were the one on the menu this evening."

Taking a sip of my Salty Dog, I reply, "That can be arranged."

Decker chuckles as a couple approaches the bar, taking the empty seats to my left. "Plans this evening?" he asks, holding my gaze.

"No plans."

"Good. I'm off at four and will run home and shower, grab a change of clothes. I thought maybe we could go to one of my favorite local restaurants this evening for dinner. Tomorrow, if you have nothing planned, I have a surprise outing."

Delight fills my chest. "I have no plans."

"Perfect. We'll head out around ten, if that works."

"It does," I confirm.

He nods before looking over to the couple seated beside me and giving them his attention. "What can I getcha to drink?"

"I'll have a Miller Lite and my wife wants to try one of those Salty Dog specials," the man says.

I glance over and meet the wife's eyes. "You'll love it," I assure her, holding up my glass and taking a drink of what's left.

"I'm excited to try it, thank you!" she replies, smiling in gratitude before turning her attention to the man making her drink.

I follow suit, watching him work and sigh in appreciation at the view. I've never been this woman, the one who openly ogles a man while he's working. Yet, when it comes to Decker, he seems to bring out a side of me I didn't even know existed. That's just one of the many things I'll miss about him when our time is up. His generosity, passion, and humor. Not to mention the fact he's the sexiest man I've ever laid eyes on, and he's nothing like any man I've ever known. The thought of returning home, being forced to be wined and dined by Jefferson Martin causes the fish in my stomach to turn.

No, that's not the life I want.

It's time for me to take control and choose my own path.

Perhaps once I've dealt with all my excess baggage, I'll be free to live on my own terms. It's a daunting thought, but a necessary one. Only when I've truly let go of the weight my name carries will I be truly free.

And *that* is what I ultimately want from this life I live.

Freedom.

Chapter SIXTEEN

Decker

"Have I told you how much I love this dress?" I ask as we enter the resort through the front entrance.

Adeline chuckles, glancing over her shoulder and meeting my heated gaze. "Yes, I believe you've told me no less than a dozen times." A blush settles into her cheeks as we walk past the front counter.

"Excuse me, Miss Montgomery. I have a message for you."

I feel her tense against me, knowing instantly it's probably another message from her father.

We walk to the front counter, and the polite woman gives her a warm smile as she hands over the envelope. She looks up at me, does a quick double take, before nodding in greeting and going about her business. Adeline sighs as we continue to the elevator and step inside.

I don't say a word, just reach out and draw her to my chest. Her hands grip my T-shirt, the familiar scent of her perfume wrapping around me. Grounding me. Calming me. I lead her off the elevator and toward her room, her keycard out and sliding into the slot the moment we reach it.

The moment the door is closed, I reach out and take the envelope. "Let's go out onto the balcony."

She nods, dropping her little purse on the table and kicking off her sandals. I open the sliding glass door and step out into the warm night air. There's a small table with two chairs to the left and a chaise lounge to the right. I opt to take a seat there and wait for Adeline to join me.

A few voices filter through the air. Some are kids playing in the pool on the ground floor around the corner, while others come from the beach out front and rooms with their doors open. We're very fortunate not to have direct neighbors to the left or right, and as far as I've been able to tell, no one is in the rooms above or below us either. I know the resort tries to spread out guests so they're not on top of each other, but I imagine it'll fill up very soon, considering there's another wedding here on Sunday afternoon.

Adeline steps out and offers me a smile before approaching the railing. All I can do is sit here and watch as she stares out at the ocean before her. There's a slight breeze playing with her hair and the full moon reflects brightly off the water. The scene gives her an almost angelic appearance, and I'm rendered positively speechless at the sight.

When she finally turns my way, there's a heaviness in her shoulders and a sadness in her eyes. Spreading my legs, I tap the space between them, inviting her to take a seat. She does, slipping onto the lounge and resting her back against my chest. I can't get over how right we fit together, like two puzzle pieces.

I hold up the envelope with one hand and softly caress her arm with the other. She exhales loudly, slowly reaching for the message. "I already know who it's from," she states.

"I figured."

She opens the sealed envelope and removes the sheet of paper. I lean forward, placing my lips to her bare shoulder as she reads the words. As much as I'd like to see what he says, I don't look. It's not my place, even though the way my heart gallops in my chest makes me feel like maybe it is.

"He's a bit more demanding now," she mutters quietly. Glancing over her shoulder, she asks, "Did you read it?"

I shake my head. "It's your message, not mine."

Her blue eyes return to the paper in her hand. "Dearest Adeline, this game you're playing has gone on long enough. There are consequences to actions deemed inappropriate and childish. Your presence is required at the office Monday morning. Eight o'clock. Don't miss this meeting."

"Love, Dad?" I joke, knowing that's not how the message ended.

"He didn't even put his name this time," she replies, dropping her hand to her lap.

I drag my lips across her shoulder once more, smiling when I see goose bumps erupt across her skin. "I'm sorry. I understand completely what it's like to have an asshole father."

She looks back at me, studying my face as she holds my gaze. I expect her to ask more questions about my own father and am surprised when she asks something on a completely different topic. "If you could have picked anything in the world to do with your life, what would you have done?"

"Easy. I was going to be a baseball player."

"Really?" she asks, her lips curling upward in a grin. "I've heard a lot about the perks of a pair of tightly fitted baseball pants."

I chuckle at her comment, running my index finger up the inside of her arm. "They were a huge hit with the girls in high school."

"That devilish grin *and* baseball pants? I bet you were very popular in school."

Nodding, I confirm, "For sure. Had to beat 'em off with a stick."

"What happened?" she asks, leaning her head back against my shoulder and relaxing.

"Blew out my shoulder in college. I wasn't going pro or anything, but I enjoyed the game. I was told there were a few farm teams interested in pursuing me, but it was never my dream to play professionally. I just wanted to get my degree, play some ball, and enjoy life, ya know?"

"What degree?"

I shift in my seat, not because I'm ashamed, but for the simple fact I never talk about this. "I have a Bachelor of Fine Arts degree."

She gazes back at me again. "Really?"

I nod, continuing to run my fingers across her soft skin. "Yeah. I wanted to be an artist."

"That's awesome."

I shrug, feeling a touch uncomfortable with the direction of the conversation, yet knowing it needs to be said. "I really enjoyed art history classes."

"That's fascinating," she says, as if me wanting to be an artist isn't unusual or just a hobby, or as my dad referred to it, as lack of ambition and a dead end. She reaches over and runs her finger across the tattoo on my forearm.

"I drew that. In fact, I drew all my tattoos," I confess.

Her eyes widen before she gazes down at the ink with renewed appreciation. "You're very talented."

"Talented at drawing, but there's no way I could actually tattoo them onto someone's skin."

"No?" she asks, her touch causing my dick to thicken in my shorts.

"No way."

She holds my gaze and asks, "Will you draw one on me?"

"A tattoo?"

Adeline nods. "Yeah."

My mind spins with ideas and the prospect of marking her perfect, smooth skin with ink. No, not tattoo ink, but another kind. "Lean forward," I instruct, slipping out from behind her and moving to her room. I know they offer pads of paper and ink pens by the desk, which I find positioned prominently in the middle of the space. Grabbing the pen, I return outside. "I'll give you an ink pen tattoo, as long as you answer my question."

She seems skeptical, but only for a moment. "All right. I'll answer whatever you want."

I nod, taking a seat at the end of the lounge. "Where do you want it?"

"I want you to give me whatever tattoo you want, wherever you feel it would work best." She meets my gaze as she adds, "I trust you."

Meaning, she knows I won't draw a dragon on her forehead or a big, hard dick across her back. She understands I'd draw something beautiful and delicate, like her, in a spot suitable for her ink. "Okay, lie down," I say, the idea coming to life.

I release the backrest of the lounge chair so it's flat and watch as she lies back. With a wicked grin, I add, "I'm going to pull up your dress."

Her blue eyes darken, and her breathing hitches. Adeline reaches down and draws her dress up around her waist, exposing a white scrap of soft lace. "Jesus, I didn't think this through," I mutter, running my hand down my face before my eyes drink in the sight lying before me in white lace panties.

She giggles. "How far do I need to pull up my dress?" she asks, humor laced in her question.

"That's fine," I tell her, spotting enough creamy flesh on her lower abdomen to serve its purpose.

I crouch down beside her, doing everything I can to keep my focus on the task at hand. It would be so easy to slip those panties down and devour her pussy, and while that's a solid idea, it'll have to wait a bit.

"You have no requests?" I confirm, clicking the pen so the point is out and ready to go.

"Nope. I want you to choose."

Nodding, I run my finger over the tip of the pen until I see ink and get to work. Adeline jumps as soon as I begin to draw. "Stop moving," I instruct with a smile.

"I'm sorry, but I'm ticklish."

"Well, hold still and I'll reward you with something dirty and orgasmic when I'm finished," I say, waggling my eyebrows suggestively.

She nods and closes her eyes, lying completely still.

"So, you know I wanted to be a baseball player and an artist. What would you be if you could choose any occupation in the world?" I ask, concentrating on my design.

"I feel bad saying this, because I've been told I would be an attorney since I was a little girl, but I didn't want to follow in my family's footsteps," she confesses, her words quiet and small.

"What did you want to be?"

She smiles, even though her eyes are still closed, as she answers, "I wanted to own a clothing boutique." Adeline opens her eyes and meets mine. "I know, silly and shallow, right?"

"There's nothing shallow or silly about that," I reply easily. "Why do you think that?"

She shrugs, and I think she's not going to answer, but then she relaxes again on the lounger and closes her eyes. "I suppose it's because of my name, the money attached to it, and the influence my family has. I should want to do something noble and life-changing like help cure cancer or solving world hunger. Instead, I picture myself working this cute little boutique with stylish, yet affordable outfits for all occasions."

All I can do is smile at her.

"I took a few clothing and textiles, as well as fashion merchandising classes during college. My father said he didn't care what electives I took, as long as I earned perfect grades and didn't soil his good name. Turns out, I really enjoyed those classes, not that I could tell him that."

I look up from my drawing and watch her face as the emotions play out. Sadness and regret are evident, and it triggers my own remorse, because I know how she feels. The only difference is I got out.

She didn't.

Deciding I need to be gentle, I keep my focus on my design and say, "You know, that's still an option."

She snorts in disagreement. "It's not, and that's okay. I've come to terms with it."

Again, I glance up and find her watching me. "When you're ready, Addi, you'll see that this life can be yours and not what someone else dictates it to be. It's not an easy step, but I promise you, you're strong enough to take back your life when you're ready. I believe in you."

Her blue eyes cloud with unshed tears, but she blinks them away. "Is that what you did?" she asks quietly.

Nodding, I state, "Yes. It wasn't easy, especially when you're controlled by someone else, but when I left, I never looked back, and I don't regret my decision at all. Well, that's not true. My only regret is the fact I wasn't there when my grandpa died. I didn't get to say goodbye in person."

"I'm sorry."

"Don't be," I insist, returning my attention to my work. "He told me not to come right before he passed because he knew my presence would cause unnecessary problems for me. A part of me wishes I would have ignored his request and gone, but I understand why he said it. He wasn't worried about anyone but me. He knew if I was there, my dad would start shit and create drama, so he told me to not come home. He asked me to find a lake or a river or a pond somewhere, wet a line, and drink a beer in his memory, so that's what I did."

Even though I can't see her face, I can feel her smile. "That sounds like a great way to honor him."

I nod. "It was fitting. He used to take me fishing all the time. It was our thing."

"I've never been," she confesses, grabbing my attention once more.

"No?" I ask, even though it's not surprising. I'd have a hard time seeing Adeline fishing. Well, the old Adeline that is. This new, more adventurous woman is always surprising me, and I smile at the thought of her enjoying fishing.

"No way. My family only does activities where you get dressed up, not down." After a few seconds, she asks, "Would I have to touch the worm?"

A chuckle draws from my gut as I work on the fine detail of her ink tattoo. "You're not a fisherman if you don't bait your own hook, Adeline. Or a fisherwoman, in your case."

She shutters. "I'm not sure I could do that."

"You might be able to talk me into baiting your hook for you, for the right price," I state suggestively.

"Well, we'll have to add taking the fish off the hook too, because I don't think I could do that either."

Laughing, I shake my head and ask, "So, you're basically holding the pole while I do all the work?"

Adeline shrugs. "I mean, it seems fair."

We're silent for a few more minutes while I add the finishing touches to her skin. When I sit back, I instantly smile at the final result. "There. Done."

"Can I see?" The excitement is evident in her voice.

"Of course," I tell her, reaching out my hand to help her stand. "Let's go in the room where the lighting is better."

Her skirt falls around her legs as we move into the room. I realize the lighting isn't that great in here either, so I escort her straight to the bathroom where the lighting isn't very flattering, but definitely brighter.

"Take off your dress, Addi," I state, my request gravelly.

She releases the zipper at her side and shimmies the little straps down her shoulders. She holds it against her chest for only a moment before letting go. My eyes watch as the bright material slowly falls down her body and pools at her feet. She's braless, which is sexy as fuck, by the way, and all I can think about is stripping those white panties from her body and bending her over the counter.

I don't, however.

Instead, I gently take her arm and move her to stand directly in front of me, facing the mirror. She's watching me through the glass, holding my gaze and waiting. My hands shift down her arms, and I'm certain I'll never feel skin as soft and amazing as hers. Finally, after what feels like an eternity, I whisper, "Go ahead and look."

Her eyes drop down to her lower abdomen, and she gasps. Her eyes fill with tears as she stares at the drawing on her skin. My heart starts to hammer in my chest as I wait for her to say something. When the wetness in her eyes starts to slide down her cheeks, I can't take it anymore. I spin her around and pull her into my arms. "What's wrong?" I ask, worried I've done something to offend her.

"It's…" She sniffles and shakes her head, trying to find the words. "Decker, it's…beautiful."

I smile and place my lips on the tip of her nose. "Just like you."

Shaking her head, she pulls back and turns around to see it once more in the mirror. "I've never seen anything so real and so breathtaking in all my life."

"I hope you know it represents you, Addi."

She wipes at the tears on her face, her eyes locked on the heart I drew. It's not just any heart. It's delicate and intricate, with many lines interlocking to create the simple shape. But it's the top that really sets off the entire piece. From one side of the heart a dozen tiny butterflies erupt from the line, as if something so simple can transform into something so glorious and free.

And that's what her ink tattoo represents.

Freedom.

When she's ready, those lines embroidered on her skin will change, transforming from her soul and taking flight.

Setting her free.

I just wish I were going to be around to watch her soar.

Chapter SEVENTEEN

Adeline

"Where are we going?" I ask as we speed up the coast to a destination unknown.

"So impatient," he replies, bringing my hand up to his lips to kiss my knuckles. "Have any of my surprises been bad?"

"No," I quickly reply, recalling the dolphin watching adventure, the private dinners, and other stops we've made in the last five days. Every one of them has been memorable.

"Well, we're almost there," he quickly adds, turning from the coastal highway and heading more inland.

"Are we going fishing?" I ask, glancing down at my gorgeous new outfit and secretly hoping that's not what we're doing. Not because I don't want to go, but my ensemble doesn't exactly call to my inner fisherman.

He glances over and down at my outfit. "Uhh, no. As much as I really appreciate what you're wearing, it would not be good for fishing."

Sighing, I scan our surroundings as we drive, looking for clues. I receive a big one as we pass a sign for an airfield up the road. My heart skips a beat at the possibilities. Are we going on a trip? Obviously, I'm leaving tomorrow, so it wouldn't be a long one, but even day trips are fun.

He pulls into a small parking lot and it's in that moment I see the sign.

Helicopter Tours

"We're going up in a helicopter?" I ask, already releasing my seat belt.

"We are. Is that okay?" He seems a little nervous now that we're here.

"Of course it is. I've flown on airplanes of all sizes, but never a helicopter. I've always wanted to do one of those island tours," I insist, recalling how I wanted to tour Hawaii and see the volcanoes.

"Well, this probably won't be as cool as an island tour, but you'll get to see the Florida coast and some private islands."

"That sounds perfect," I insist, reaching for the door handle. "Let's go."

I'm out before he is, and I can hear his chuckle until the moment I shut the passenger door. He grabs a bag from the back seat of his car and joins me at the hood. Decker takes my hand and leads me toward the office. Before we step inside, he turns me to face him and wraps his arms around my waist. "You look absolutely edible in this two-piece outfit."

Of course the compliment makes me grin immediately. "Thank you."

"*When* you start your own boutique, I hope you carry things like this in it," he insists, trailing his finger across the elastic at the waist of the pants.

"*If* I start my own boutique, it will be filled with stylish and affordable pieces that anyone can purchase. So many of the places I shop cater only to those with a huge credit card limit, and I wouldn't want that. It should be an experience for everyone, not just the rich," I tell him. I've dreamed about this since I was twenty years old, and even though this pipe dream will never come to fruition, I've put a lot of thought into what I'd want to sell.

He leans forward and kisses my nose. "*When*, sweet Adeline. Now, come on. Let's go for a ride."

The next thirty minutes are spent filling out forms and signing liability waivers, deeming the company not responsible if anything should happen, including death. I try not to think about the clause, telling myself you'll never experience all life has to offer if you're scared to take a risk. Finally, we're led to a large hangar to be given our pre-flight instructions.

A young woman appears with a warm smile on her face. "Good morning. I'm Abigail, your pilot and tour guide. We're taking a thirty-minute flight today, and the weather is absolutely perfect for sightseeing," she boasts before glancing down at my feet. "Oh, wait. You're not able to wear sandals."

Dread causes my stomach to drop because I didn't plan accordingly. In fact, I didn't plan at all since I wasn't aware of today's adventure, but I can't help the overwhelming feeling of disappointment.

"We're good. I brought her shoes," Decker says, setting the bag on the floor.

My heart jumps in my chest and tears fill my eyes as I watch him pull out a light jacket, hair clip, ankle socks, and a pair of shoes from the bag.

"Perfect," Abigail proclaims. "I'll give you a few minutes to change your shoes and get ready, and then we'll go over the safety instructions."

She turns and walks away, but my eyes are on the magnificent man in front of me. Not only did he decide to take me on another once in a lifetime adventure, but he brought all the necessary things I'd need so he could keep it a surprise.

"How did you know?" I whisper, a large lump forming in my throat and making it difficult to breathe.

"Well, when I booked the tour yesterday, they gave me a list of things we'd need. When I ran home to shower and get a change of clothes, I stopped at the store and bought you a pair of shoes, since I didn't see anything closed toe in your room. Plus, they say darker clothes are better to avoid glares and it could be a bit windy, so I grabbed a thick black jacket for you to slip on over your top. And even though you'll be wearing a helmet, I thought you may want to pull your hair back," he says, holding up the elastic tie as if it's no big deal.

But it's a huge deal.

No one has ever treated me the way he does. Like I'm valued, and not just because of my name or social status. He treats me with respect, dignity, and as if I'm an equal, not a bother. It's in this moment I realize I'm falling in love with him. Not just caring for the man I've known for a week, but actually falling. He's the most caring, patient, respectful man I've ever known, and the idea of renting a car in the morning and driving home to South Carolina sits in my chest with the weight of a thousand bricks.

It's suddenly very hard to breathe.

"Hey, are you okay?" he asks, a worried look on his face.

"Yes," I whisper, blinking rapidly to keep the tears at bay. No way do I want to cry like a baby now and ruin what's left of our time together. I have one day left, and I'm going to cherish every second. Clearing my throat, I add, "Sorry, I just really appreciate you thinking of me." Reaching for the hair tie, I pull my hair back in a low ponytail at the base of my neck.

He gives me a soft smile, one that still makes his face light up brilliantly, but holds a hint of sadness, as if maybe he knows exactly what sorrow fills my mind and understands it completely.

"Still want to go?"

I'm already nodding before he even finishes the sentence. "Definitely. Let me change my shoes, and then I'll be ready."

Decker holds out the socks, which I slip onto my feet, and eventually the shoes. I own a pair of athletic shoes back at home in my penthouse condo, but those are only used for the occasional yoga class I'm invited to by other ladies at the country club.

This pair has elastic instead of a traditional shoelace you'd tie, and I find them extremely comfortable. "Thank you for these. Dare I ask how you knew my size?"

He grins widely and winks. "A gentleman never tells."

"I'm sure it was a challenge to find my size. Tall women have unfortunate big feet," I mutter, repeating something I've heard my mother say throughout my life.

When I was in seventh grade, I shot past all my classmates, including the boys. I reached my five-ten height by the time I was a freshman in high school, and Mother frequently expressed her displeasure at having a tall daughter instead of the petite five-three or five-four girls her friends all had. It was as if my height was somehow my fault and not at all thanks to the genetics she and my father provided me.

I've always wondered where my height comes from. My mom is a tiny, petite thing, and while my dad is a larger than life, powerful South Carolina lawyer, he barely stands over my height. In fact, with the exception of sharing my mother's blue eyes and blond hair, I look more like the pool boy's kid than my own father's.

"There's nothing wrong with the size of your feet, Adeline," he counters, taking a step forward and crowding my personal space. "I personally like every little detail about you. You're just the right size for me."

I feel my cheeks heat up, recalling how well we fit together for being only a few inches different in height. "I agree."

"Good," he says, kissing the tip of my nose. "Now, come on. Let's go up in a helicopter."

"Without a doubt, best day ever," I proclaim once we're back at the hangar.

"You haven't stopped smiling," he replies with his own grin on his face.

"You either," I insist, slipping off the shoes and socks and putting my wedge sandals back on.

"Because today has been remarkable, and the best part is, it's still early. How about we go to lunch?"

"Sounds good," I say, pulling my hair out of the elastic tie and wishing I had a brush. I can't imagine how terrible my hair looks from wearing the helmet, and I'm sure there's a crinkle in my hair from being pulled back.

"Here."

I look over at Decker and he's holding a black plastic comb. "Did I look that bad?" I quip, noting his hair, while still mussed, looks like it's supposed to be styled that way. He looks positively delicious with his bed-head appearance.

"Absolutely not," he insists, "but I know how girls are. Plus, tangles are the worst."

Taking the comb, I start to gently run it through my hair, pleasantly surprised it's not as knotted as I expect. "You seem to think of every-thing. Are you sure you're not secretly married?"

His smile falls as he turns his complete attention my way. "Hell no. I'd never cheat on a spouse, nor would I lead you on and deceive you like that."

Comb all but forgotten, I place my hands on his chest and step forward. "I know that. I was teasing, really. I promise."

He relaxes and nods. "Okay. Good. Sorry for overreacting, but I don't want you to think I'd ever do something like that."

"I don't." And that's the truth. What I've discovered about Decker Paulson over the last week doesn't align with someone who would intentionally deceive me like that. Yes, I'm certain there are plenty of men out there who would, swearing they're single and bedding women for pleasure, and then going home to the little wife and kids. But I've seen where he lives, and I've already determined he's not like any man I've ever known.

My hands move to his arms, my fingers dancing up his warm, tanned skin before slipping under the sleeves of his black T-shirt. The ink is there, so beautiful and fitting, and that makes me wonder...

"Can I ask you a question?" My eyes are focused on the dark black lines of his tattoo.

"Of course."

Swallowing hard, I finally look up and meet his soulful brown gaze. "Do you think I would look okay with a tattoo?" His face registers shock, so before he can say anything, I go on. "Not anything big or viewable when you see me, but I don't know, maybe something small, hidden away from the world. Something that's only for me." My eyes drop to his chest.

Decker places his thumb beneath my chin and angles my face up. He's wearing a big smile as he says, "I think a tattoo on your delicate skin would be the sexiest thing in the world. Especially if it's hidden away, only viewed by someone who gets to see you so intimately."

I can't help but smile, because in all my life, I've never thought of marking my skin in such a fashion, yet now, it's all I can think about.

Clearing my throat, I ask the second part of my request. "Okay, well, then I have one more question for you. Would you draw it? The heart and butterflies? I'd like to tattoo that in the same spot you drew your design last night."

Unfortunately, the pen ink didn't survive our joint shower last night and is nearly gone this morning after a second shower to get ready for today's adventure. I couldn't believe how sad I felt when I looked down and it was washed away. The idea hit me hard while standing in front of the mirror, and all I could think about was permanently putting it back on my skin.

"You want me to draw you a tattoo?" His words are hoarse and dripping with emotion.

"Yes."

He opens his mouth, but nothing comes out right away. I give him a few moments, hoping he's not trying to come up with a way to let me down easy. It's not that it's a huge ask, but it seems like a very personal one, so I can understand him hesitating.

"I'd be honored to draw you a tattoo, Addi," he says softly, pulling me into his arms and squeezing me tightly.

Relief washes over me. I'm a bit nervous to have needles stabbing into my skin, especially something as permanent as a tattoo, but knowing the markings will be something he drew, well, that helps settle the tension in my stomach. "Thank you."

"Do you have a studio in mind?"

I chuckle uneasily. "Oh. Well, I kind of forgot about that part. I guess I didn't even think about who would do the tattoo and if they were available before I leave tomorrow."

He pulls out his phone—the same one he took dozens of pictures with when we were on the helicopter tour. "Let me make a call, okay?"

I nod as he taps on the screen and brings the phone to his ear. "Hey, Drake, how are ya?" He listens for a second before laughing. "Listen, the reason I'm calling is to ask a favor. Any chance you have availability today for a tattoo? I have a friend in town who'd like me to draw her a piece, nothing too big." Again, he listens before glancing over at me and narrowing his eyes. "Yes, a woman. No, I'm not giving you her number."

My eyes widen, though I'm not concerned. I know Decker wouldn't hand over my phone number to another man, and it's confirmed again the moment he starts to speak again.

"Not happening, my friend. In fact, I think I'm going to call someone else. I don't want your grubby hands anywhere near—" Decker smiles, listening to the man on the other end of the phone. "Perfect, see you then."

He taps the screen and slides the phone back into his pocket. "We're going to meet him at his studio at two. That's before he opens, but he owes me a favor, so he's willing to do it."

"Do I want to know what favor?"

He shrugs and reaches for my hand. "I helped him draw a particularly tough tattoo about four months ago, and my payment was time in his chair on a future piece. He's paying up."

"Wow, I can't believe I'm really going to do this." Suddenly, it hits me I'm actually going to ink my body, but not because I'm afraid. Because this is completely unlike me, or at least unlike the version of me I've always been.

Worry creases the skin around his eyes. "You don't have to go through with this if you don't want to. I can call Drake back and tell him never mind."

"No, it's not that," I quickly assure him. "I'm ready to get this tattoo, honestly. I just didn't think past asking you to redraw it to the actual work part. I'm relieved you were able to find someone on such short notice to help me."

He nods, making sure everything is back in the bag and taking my hand to exit the building. "Drake did this one," he says, pointing to the ink on his forearm. It looks almost tribal, with intricate detail and beautiful lines. "I'd never take you to a place I wouldn't go myself."

"I know." And I do.

I trust him completely.

"Okay, let's go get lunch and then we can head over to his place. It's about a thirty-minute drive," he says, leading me to his car.

"Sounds perfect."

Before I can slip in the passenger seat, he pulls me against his body and places his lips against mine. The kiss is gentle and unhurried and makes my toes curl in the best way. All I can do is grip the sleeves of his T-shirt and enjoy the ride, because unfortunately, the end is drawing near.

The sand is running out of the hourglass.

Our time together is drawing to a close.

"Come on, Addi. Let's go eat. If we have time, we can stop at the beach and look for seashells."

I can't help but smile. Lunch in a cozy little mom-and-pop restaurant and a walk on the beach, looking for shells with the man I'm falling in love with. "Sounds perfect."

It really does.

Chapter EIGHTEEN

Decker

"Ready?" I ask, sitting in the chair beside Adeline and watching as she prepares to get her first tattoo.

She nods and squeezes my hand a little tighter. Adeline is in the chair, the top half lying back so she's flat. The design I drew is already transferred onto her skin, and Drake is prepped and ready to go.

"All right, Adeline, you're going to hear the buzzing sound of the gun now," Drake says before turning it on.

She jerks the moment the noise fills the room. When she meets my eyes, she asks, "It's going to hurt, isn't it." It's not a question.

"Well, I'll be honest, Addi, it's not going to tickle, but the pain is only temporary. As soon as he's done, you'll feel relief. Promise."

She nods again, squeezing my hand even harder this time. Then, she pushes away her fear and grabs her resolve by the balls. "I'm ready."

Drake pulls his glasses down onto his nose and positions the tray of ink right by his side. He places his hand on her lower abdomen and leans closer. He's lucky I don't punch him in the balls for being so damn close to Adeline's body. He must sense my irritation, because he glances over at me and grins before firing up the gun. "Here we go. It'll be over soon."

The moment the needle touches her skin, she flinches, but immediately settles herself down. "You're doing great," I tell her, holding her gaze.

She grins, even though it doesn't completely meet her eyes. "It's been seven seconds, Decker."

A wide smile spreads across my mouth. "Yes, and you're doing great for seven whole seconds."

"So tell me what this tattoo means. Why did you choose it?" Drake asks. I know what he's doing. He's getting her mind off the buzzing of the needle and the discomfort it causes as he inks her flawless skin.

Holding my eyes, she gives me a private smile and says, "It means freedom."

Drake continues to work, wiping off the extra black ink as he goes. I want to watch him do his thing, because it's spectacular to watch him create art, but I don't want to look away from Adeline. She's holding it together beautifully, but I can see the uneasiness in her eyes.

"I like it," Drake replies, appreciating the meaning of the design. "So, Adeline, black butterflies or colored?"

Her eyes widen as she gapes up at me. "I don't know."

Drake, as if sensing her distress, pauses and says, "I think it'd look amazing in all black, just like the stencil Decker drew, but if you add color to the butterflies as they soar, that might really set it off."

She nods in understanding and returns her attention to me. "What do you think?"

"I think you should do what you want to do. Both options look fucking badass."

She grins before closing her eyes and taking a deep breath. "I think I want color in the butterflies."

"Any particular color or colors?"

When she opens her eyes, she looks over at the man inking her skin. "You're the artist. I trust you."

Drake looks up and nods. "I've got you, Adeline. No worries, sweetheart."

She squeezes my hand and Drake returns to his work. All I can do is watch her. She's simply stunning. More beautiful than in my wildest dreams, strong, and courageous. Not to mention loyal as hell, if her loyalty to her family is still there after all this time. I've only known her for a week and I can tell they treat her like shit. No, I'm not talking about the fancy clothes, the jewelry, or the elaborate vacations. They do that more for themselves than for her. Because their name means more than allowing their only daughter to find her own happiness.

Over the next forty-five minutes, I steal glances at his work and smile as the final result takes shape. Drake was right. The color really sets off the tattoo, and I can't wait for Adeline to see it.

Finally, after what feels like hours, Drake sits up and stretches his back, turning off the gun. "All done." He wipes the tattoo down and glances up at Adeline, a smile on his face as he asks, "Ready to see it?"

She nods eagerly, and with my help, stands up. She walks to the full-length mirror on the wall and gasps. I'm right there, cataloging her reactions and watching for any sign of distress, but I never see any. Her face transforms into pure happiness as she stares at the small tattoo. "Oh my goodness," she whispers, tears falling down her cheeks. "I've never seen anything so beautiful."

Stepping forward, I place a kiss on her lips and mutter a weak, "Me either." Only I'm not talking about the tattoo.

She meets my gaze, and I'm certain she understands what I mean. She gives me the softest smile before throwing her arms around my neck. I know her lower left abdomen will be tender if she rubs against it, so I try not to pull her against my body the way I'd like. Instead, I just hold her, mindful of her new ink, and breathe her in. I memorize the way she feels against me, because our time together is running out.

By this time tomorrow, she'll be home in South Carolina, and I'll be here.

Alone.

"How 'bout you, man? You gettin' one too?"

I glance over at Drake, a little taken back by his question. Before I can reply, Adeline is speaking, her tear-filled eyes bright with eagerness. "You can get one too?"

"Well, I hadn't planned on it," I state.

Drake shrugs. "I've got time. We don't open for another hour and a half, and the first appointment isn't until five. Up to you."

My mind starts to spin with possibilities. All the designs that have filtered through my head over the last several years all play out, but none seem fitting. There's only a short amount of time, and most of the pieces I'd want would take longer than what's allotted.

But then something new pops into my head. As I stare into Adeline's ocean-blue eyes, a design takes shape, and the urge to put pen to paper grabs hold.

"He's designing," Drake announces with a smirk. "I'll clean up the chair and get ready."

I turn to Adeline, who seems positively ecstatic to witness me getting ink. "You don't mind hanging around for a little while longer? I don't have to get one today."

"Are you kidding me? Of course I'll wait. I want to see the process, and I think it's only fair, considering you just held my hand through my tattoo."

"You're going to hold my hand?" I ask, grinning from ear to ear.

"If the situation warrants it, yes, but something tells me you don't need some woman offering you support to get another tattoo," she states, shaking her head.

I take a step closer and place my hands on her bare arms. Leaning in, I say, "You're not *some woman,* Addi."

She licks her lips anxiously and places her hands on my chest. "Who am I?" she asks.

You're everything.

But that's the one statement I can't say. I have one night left with her, and while I want to speak the truth, I still have to protect myself. And her. I can't tell her I'm falling for her and have been probably since the moment I first saw her last Friday night. There's no future for us, not with living states away. Yes, as Todd pointed out, I could easily relocate anywhere I wanted, but the thought of leaving Marian doesn't feel right either.

And there's the fact this week was supposed to be just that: One week. No strings, just sex. Those are the terms we set, and that's what I'll stick to. Even if it hurts like hell to watch her drive away tomorrow morning, I'll do it. I just hope I've created enough memories to last me the rest of my life, because something tells me Adeline Montgomery isn't going to be easy to forget.

"You're someone who is incredibly special to me," I tell her honestly.

She gives me a smile and squeezes my arms. "You're special to me too."

I place my lips against hers, savoring the feel and taste of her. "Okay, I better get drawing. We don't have much time," I tell her.

Adeline takes a seat in the chair I once occupied, while I move to the counter and start my design. It comes together quickly, and when Drake returns with a fresh tray of supplies, I'm adding the final touches. He cleans the chair before taking the pad of paper and checking out my drawing. "Nice. I'll go put it on transfer paper, and we'll get started."

I pull my T-shirt off, already knowing where this one is going. "Wow, I get a show too?" Adeline quips, making me chuckle.

"That comes later," I assure her with a wink before taking my place on the flat chair.

Drake returns with the stencil and sits beside me, handing me a mirror. "Where we putting this bad boy?" he asks. I point to my heart, directly below the one I have for my grandpa, and hold completely still as he brings the thin paper to my chest. "Here?"

"Yep," I reply, watching as he places the transfer on my skin and pats it down.

The moment he removes the stencil, I hear a gasp from the woman sitting at my side. I look to my right and see her eyes filling with tears once more as she gazes down at what I came up with. After a few seconds, she looks up at me, her mouth slightly agape. She doesn't say a word, just bends down and rests her head against my shoulder, the wetness of her tears cooling my skin.

"Don't cry, Addi," I whisper, knowing this won't be the last time I say those words. This woman is emotional, but not overly so. When she's comfortable, she drops her hard shield and lets herself feel, experiencing things she may not typically allow for herself. She must be calm, cool, and unaffected so much, it's refreshing to see herself letting go of that side and just living.

She looks up and I can't help but wipe away the wetness trailing down her face. The moment I push away one tear, another falls in its place, so I just reach for her hand and hold on tight as Drake begins the tattoo. The sting of the needle is familiar and welcome, a reminder I'm alive and able to do what I want.

My heart breaks when I realize what I really want is to see where this thing with Adeline could go.

But we don't get everything we want.

That's a painful truth.

"Coloring?" Drake asks as he is nearing the end of the outline.

"Blues. Lots of blues," I tell him. The color will forever remind me of Adeline's eyes.

When Drake is finished with my new piece, he sits back and smiles proudly as he wipes it down. "It's definitely unique, man. Pretty bad ass, if you ask me."

I don't say a word, just reach for the hand mirror so I can see the finished product. When I lay eyes on it, my throat closes and my ability to breathe becomes almost nonexistent. All I can do is stare at my new tattoo and grin, knowing what it represents and how perfect it is.

The ocean waves are vibrant blues, sapphires and turquoise mixing together beautifully. Above the crashing waves is a set of helicopter blades looking so realistic, as if they're moving through the air and truly spinning on my skin. And jumping over them is a dolphin. If you look closely, it's wearing the same wave necklace I bought for Adeline earlier in the week. The one she has worn every day since.

"Cool?" he asks, watching me check out the tattoo.

"Perfect, man. Thanks."

Drake nods happily and turns to grab ointment, spreading it generously across my smarted skin before covering it with a bandage. Once he's happy it's ready, he moves to reclean the chair and his supplies, while I grab my T-shirt and slip it back over my head.

"How much?" I ask.

He waves off my question. "Your money's no good here. We're even."

I nod and extend my hand. "Thanks, man. Appreciate you coming in early to do these for us."

"No problem. It's an honor," he replies.

Adeline steps forward and gives Drake a hug. "Thank you so much. I love my tattoo. It's perfect."

He returns the gesture and smiles. "You're very welcome. You ever want another, just give me a call. You don't even have to come with that guy," he says, nodding toward me.

She giggles in reply and steps back. I instantly reach for her hand and entwine our fingers together. "I'll keep that in mind."

He leads us through the shop and unlocks the front entrance as two women approach. "Good timing," Drake says. "Guys, this is Ash, our front desk clerk, and Jazzy, our resident piercer."

"Nice to meet you," I greet the women as we step outside.

"Let me know if you have any issues," Drake says, handing over a sheet of paper to Adeline. "Care guide for the next week. Call the number on the bottom if you have any problems."

Adeline nods. "Thank you."

Then, together, we walk toward my car with the late afternoon Florida sun beating down on us. "Where to now?" I ask when I open the passenger door.

"Is it possible to go back to the beach to collect a few more seashells?"

"Of course," I tell her, stepping back as she slides inside the car. "Wanna go back to the beach we were at or walk along the one in front of the resort?"

"Let's go back to the resort," she suggests. "Maybe we can walk down to the pier."

"Sounds good. The public beaches will be crazy-busy this time of day, and even though the one in front of the resort is still public, a lot of people avoid the area because of the extra tourists."

"Perfect," she says, adjusting the elastic of her pants so it's not rubbing against her covered tattoo.

I slip into the driver's seat and buckle up, ignoring the discomfort of the belt rubbing against my own ink, and take us back to the resort. No words are spoken, but the moment doesn't warrant them. We're both comfortable just sitting here, watching our surroundings, and being lost in our own thoughts.

My thoughts are of the woman beside me, and the fact our time together is down to about eighteen hours. In that time, I already know I won't be doing much sleeping. We'll walk on the beach, collect seashells, enjoy dinner either in her room or down in the restaurant, and hopefully make love until we're both sated and too exhausted to move.

Even then, I know it'll never be enough.

When we reach the resort, I pull into the employee lot and park near the back. With another wedding happening Sunday, the resort is filling up for the weekend, so I'd rather leave the main lot for guests who need it.

As soon as we step out of the car, music fills the air, along with the taste of the salty ocean. Of all the places I've lived, this may be my favorite. Nothing beats the view and the warm feel of the sea and sun kissing your skin.

"Where's that coming from?" Adeline asks the moment she steps out of the car.

"The tiki bar. We have live music Fridays and Saturdays. There are a lot of local artists that will sign up to play a few hours at a time. It's great exposure for them and gives them an opportunity to hone their craft."

She nods and looks back at the bag in the back seat from earlier today. "Should we run that up now?"

"Let's go look for shells first. I can grab it on our way up to the room." I pause at the trunk and retrieve the department store bag I found stuffed in there earlier that we used to collect shells at our earlier stop.

"Okay," she replies, taking my hand and walking with me through the parking lot toward the beach.

The moment we reach the sand, she slips off her sandals, leaving them to dangle from her other hand. I take off my own athletic shoes and socks, leaving them near the walkway not far from other pairs left by beach walkers.

The water is cool and very welcomed as we slowly make our way along the water's edge, letting the surf coat our legs. The pants of her outfit wet instantly, but she doesn't seem to mind. I almost suggest we go upstairs so she can change, but that idea flies out the window the moment I realize if we go up to her room, we won't be leaving anytime soon. I have plans for later.

Naked plans.

And it involves neither one of us leaving her bed until the last possible second.

Chapter NINETEEN

Adeline

We slowly stroll along the beach, picking up a few of the shells I see—leaving plenty for others to find—and even grab a couple pieces of trash to dispose of properly when we get back. As we near the pier, I glance down and find something in the sand. Upon closer inspection, I pull up a small shell, swiping it through the water to clean off the debris.

Holding it up, I'm surprised to see the detail. It's unlike anything I've ever seen. The ivory shell has dark golden spots on it and is small enough to fit in the palm of my hand.

"Wow, I think that's a Junonia shell. They're incredibly rare."

I glance over at Decker and hand over the seashell for him to inspect. "What makes them rare?"

"Well, according to Marian, who has given me a lesson or two on coastal seashells, these house Junonia snails that live in deep water. The snail has to die and detach, and then the shell is brought to shore by strong currents from a storm or something. It's pretty fascinating," he informs me, spinning the shell around before handing it back to me.

I shake my head. "You keep it."

He seems genuinely surprised. "Me? Why?"

I place the small shell back in his hand, cupping my palm over it so it's enclosed. "To remember me by."

He puts down the bag of shells in the sand and cups my cheeks in his big, warm hands. "Forgetting you isn't a possibility, Addi. You'll always be on my mind," he says, swallowing hard before adding, "and in my heart."

My own throat works to allow oxygen to pass through my airways. "Same, Decker."

He smiles sweetly and slips the shell into his pocket before grabbing the bag and reaching for my hand. "Ready to head back to the resort? We can decide on dinner."

I nod, ready to go back to the room and begin the next phase of our evening. I'm certain it'll involve way less clothing and a few orgasms.

As we start walking back, he asks, "Do you want to have dinner at the restaurant?"

"No, I think I'd prefer to stay in," I reply suggestively, making him smile.

"I like the way you think, Addi."

We make our way back to the resort silently, and my eyes take it all in. The people, the view, the man walking beside me. It's all part of it, this exceptional trip that may have started off a little sketchy—well, everything but getting to hang out with my friend Audrey and the girls—and has transformed into something I'll never forget.

As we reach the walkway, Decker picks up his shoes before guiding me through the sliding doors of the resort. The air-conditioning is welcome but cold against my wet pants that cling to my calves. The front counter is busy with check-ins, and the restaurant to the right has a small group waiting outside the doors for a table. The bar isn't nearly as active yet, but I'm certain it will be soon.

"I think I need to warm up in the shower," I say, a shiver sweeping through my limbs.

He looks my way and grins mischievously. "I'm certain I can come up with a way or two to warm you right up."

I spin to face him, slowly walking backward as we make our way to the elevator. "I believe I'd like to hear about these ways, Mr. Paulson," I tease. "There *is* this thing you do with your tongue that I—"

"Adeline."

My entire body freezes as the voice registers. Slowly, I turn around and come face-to-face with the one man I wasn't expecting to see.

My father.

"Wh-what are you doing here?" I ask, my voice suddenly small and shaky.

"I came to collect my daughter," he states firmly, his eyes driving into Decker.

I feel Decker's gaze move to me, but I can't stop staring at the older man in front of me. His temples appear a bit less gray, which tells me he's been to the salon very recently, and his hazel eyes a familiar mixture of disappointment and agitation.

My father takes a step closer, immediately causing me to take one back. Not because I believe he'd hurt me. Oh, no. Edward Montgomery isn't one to hurt you physically. He'd destroy you in other ways. Your reputation, finances, and probably a few ways I don't want to know about.

"It's well past time you return home, Adeline."

"Excuse me," Decker says, inserting himself between my father and me. "I'm Decker, Adeline's friend. And you must be?"

My father finally turns to give Decker his attention. "I know who you are, Mr. Paulson."

If Decker is surprised, he doesn't show it, just extends his hand for the great Edward Montgomery to shake. My father just looks at his hand, as if it were dirty or a bug that might attack him.

"Adeline, your stay here is ov—"

"Perhaps this conversation could be had in private?" Decker insists, interrupting my father politely, yet leaving no room for argument that this discussion shouldn't happen in the lobby of the resort.

It's the first time I've noticed a few guests lingering, listening to our conversation and waiting for the altercation. I'm surprised phones aren't out, ready to catch all the action. "We can go up to my room," I suggest, but my father is already shaking his head.

"I'm not going up to your room, Adeline," he argues, a look of disgust on his face. As if my room is somehow scandalous or dirty.

"We can use one of the small private dining rooms. I don't believe they're all in use tonight," Decker offers, pointing toward the other large hallway away from the lobby. He takes my hand and gives it a gentle squeeze as we lead the way. "You okay?" he whispers, undoubtedly understanding how upsetting this surprise visit has made me.

I nod, unable to find the right words to even respond. Am I okay? Physically, yes, but I know his presence here isn't going to end well.

Ironically, the available room Decker leads us to is the same one we met in last Friday night. The one from Audrey's rehearsal dinner, and something tells me these new memories won't be as great as the first ones made here.

The moment we're inside, my father turns to Decker. "I will speak to my daughter alone. This is a family matter."

He turns to look at me, as if seeking my decision on the matter. If I want him to stay, I know, without a doubt, he would. But he also understands I may need to have this conversation alone. He won't like it, but he'll understand.

I nod, letting him know it's okay to leave. I want to tell him he can go upstairs and wait for me in my room, but I'm certain that's fruitless. Decker confirms it when he replies, "I'll be right outside the door." He gives my father a pointed look before slowly moving to the door and closing it behind him.

The silence in the room is deafening, and the temperature seems to have dropped thanks to the icy stare directed my way, but I hold my head up high and stand as straight as possible. "Why are you here?" I ask, not wanting to beat around the bush.

He seems taken aback by my question. Considering he's made his career by schooling his expressions and only showing emotion when it benefits him before a jury, that's saying something. "Why? Because my daughter has decided to traipse around with a man she doesn't know, ignoring her obligations and commitments."

"I know Decker," is the response I give, knowing it'll heckle on his nerves more than work.

He scoffs. "Do you? You know about his arrest record? How about how his father is suing him for breach of contract? Or that he's on the run, which would explain why he moves from location to location every six months to a year? He's shared all his dirty details with you, right? I'm sure it made for great pillow talk when your legs are no longer in the air."

A gasp flies from my lips.

"Oh, don't pretend that's not what this is. You're a gorgeous young lady, and I know exactly how men are when they see a woman like you. Rich, beautiful. I just didn't think you were the type to sleep with random guys you doesn't know. Apparently, you're more like your mother than I thought."

My jaw is practically unhinged as I stare at him. Not only is he calling me a whore, but my mother too? I don't even know what to say at this moment, but the realization is abruptly clear. I don't want this life. I don't want to be controlled by a man who'd so easily cast his daughter aside while she's building a career—the same career he insisted she have. Who would so blatantly and effortlessly disregard her feelings and refer to her as a promiscuous woman, as if she were sleeping with a dozen guys while on vacation instead of one.

But what hurts the most is the fact he doesn't know me, nor does he care to. My father wants what my father wants, and he doesn't care who he hurts to get it.

"Since you seem to be at a loss for words right now, you'll listen. You will be returning with me to Charleston within the hour. You have a meeting planned for eight tomorrow morning with the partners, where you will apologize for your rude behavior and promise to mind your P's and Q's for the foreseeable future. You will support Ethan Hatherley by assisting him with his big case, and not act like a child. Seriously, Adeline. I thought we raised you better than that."

My eyes have to be bugging out from my head. *You raised me better than that?* You didn't raise me at all! I was raised by a nanny, and only to be seen or heard from when absolutely necessary. I was an inconvenience. A pawn from the get-go. Something bright and shiny they could show off at special events.

The clarity is so vivid, so engulfing, it's overwhelming, but somehow, I manage to reply, "I'm not going back."

"You are," he replies pointedly.

"No, I'm staying."

This time, he laughs, only it doesn't hold an ounce of humor. "I don't think you understand, dear daughter. You *will* return with me. No daughter of mine will be shacking up with a criminal, getting tattoos and ignoring her responsibilities. Think of the smear campaign they'd use against me when I run for office, Adeline. Your family legacy could be ruined, and it would be your fault.

"No, you will come back. If you don't, I'll make one phone call that will ruin your new *friend's* life. He wants to run and hide from his own family, well, that's on him, but he will not take you down with him." He adjusts his necktie as he calmly adds, "I'm a very powerful man. One phone call and your friend would spend the rest of his life behind bars."

My stomach drops to my feet as cold dread fills my entire body. I've never personally witnessed this vindictive side of my father, but I have no doubt he's every bit as mean as I imagine he'd be. If he wants to mess with Decker's life, he will. His resources are endless, and his threat to ruin the man I've come to love, he will make it his life's mission until he achieves the goal.

Realization sets in, and my choices aren't choices at all.

Sure, I can stay, but for how long? The moment I defy him, he'll already have his plan in motion. He'll ruin Decker, and I can't let that happen. He means too much to me to allow that to happen when he's finally free himself. I won't let my father send him right back to his own father, especially when he worked so hard to get away and live his own life.

I refuse to be the one who tosses him to the wolves.

"I don't know why you're doing this," I whisper, the most intense wave of sadness settling into my chest.

"Because I will protect my name and legacy with everything I have," he states, adjusting the gold and black onyx cuff links on his shirt.

"You could let me go," I tell him, feeling as if I have to offer the suggestion, even though I already know what his answer will be.

"You will return to Charleston with me. You will apologize as I've instructed, and then we will be attending the dinner with Jefferson and push your relationship forward. The plan has always been for you to marry him. If not, I will make one phone call to Decker's father and get the ball rolling on his end. Decker will be home and paying for his crimes within hours of that phone call, daughter. The choice is yours."

No, there is no choice at all.

I'd never allow him to hurt and destroy Decker, even if that means I go back to South Carolina and never look back. The thought makes me nauseous, but what other choice do I have? I won't allow my father to hurt Decker for spite.

I will go.

To protect him.

"Fine."

"You have exactly fifteen minutes to pack your things. I will be in the car. Don't be late." And with that, he heads for the door and exits the room.

"Are you all right?" Decker asks, entering the space as soon as my father is through the door. He pulls me into his arms, and the familiar scent of his bodywash and detergent hits me. I'm unable to stop the tears as they start to spill. I cling to him like a lifeline, refusing to think about the fact this will be the last time he holds me. "Addi?"

"I'm okay," I whisper, even though it may be a lie.

I won't ever be okay again.

He pulls back and takes stock over my features. There's an anguish reflecting in his eyes, one I feel deep in my soul. "Tell me what happened."

I take a deep breath, knowing our time has run out.

This is goodbye.

"I need to go," I tell him, trying to muster all the bravado I can.

"Now?"

I nod, wishing it weren't so. "Yes."

He exhales and searches my face. "Are you sure? You could stay until tomorrow, like planned. I know you were going to rent a car, but I could drive you. I'm sure I could easily trade a few days with other employees to give myself about a week," he suggests, and even though I want nothing more than to take him up on the offer, I know I can't.

"I'm sure," I state, swallowing the bile rising in my throat. "I have obligations waiting for me."

He doesn't say a word. In fact, when he opens his mouth, I expect him to argue. He's aware of my obligations, but also knows the other side. The fact that I don't want them. For me to be telling him I must go because of them is certain to cause him confusion. "Addi," he starts, but I cut him off. I have to.

"My father is waiting for me," I quickly interject.

He nods, almost woodenly. "All right, if you're sure."

Am I sure?

No, I'm not sure at all.

I want Decker. I want to stay here, with him.

But images of my father reaching out to Decker's dad and causing problems for him are front and center in my mind, and I know my father will do whatever he can to make Decker's life hell.

And I love him too much to let that happen.

"I'm sure." I paste on one of the fake grins I've been wearing my entire life, praying he doesn't see through it.

With another nod, he takes my hand, collects the shoes that were dropped onto the floor when we entered the room—I was so surprised to see my father, I didn't even realize I wasn't holding them anymore— and slowly make our way up to my room. The elevator ride is silent, discomfort and displeasure so heavy in the air it's stifling.

Stepping inside my room isn't any better. If anything, it's worse. My eyes move to the bed where we were supposed to spend all the hours I have left before I leave, but now those hours are gone. What's left is minutes, and minutes pass you by so fast, you barely have time to savor them.

I already know what little bit of time I have now won't be long enough.

It'll never be enough.

"I'll help you pack," he offers, going to the closet and retrieving my suitcases, and all I can do is watch.

When those minutes are up and it's time for me to go, I'm not taking everything with me.

I'm leaving my heart behind.

Chapter TWENTY

Decker

This is hell.

Pure torturous hell.

Packing her belongings so she can leave is not what I had in mind for this evening. We haven't had dinner, maybe a final walk on the beach. I haven't gotten to make love to her until we're both boneless and so damn exhausted we fall asleep entangled in each other's arms, only to awake after a couple hours of sleep to do it all over again.

That's what I had in store for this evening.

Nowhere in my plans was the idea of her packing up and leaving early, and I'm certain it wasn't her plan either.

I still don't understand what's going on, but I'm not sure I'm in any position to push her for more information. Our agreement has always been for this...*thing* between us to end when she returned home, so why the fuck am I so upset because she's doing exactly what she said she would?

Because she's leaving early, and the circumstances scream fishy as fuck?

Or how about because you're in love with her now, making the thought of her leaving that much more traumatic?

Yeah, definitely both of them.

I move silently through the room as Adeline haphazardly shoves things into the suitcases. Since she stayed longer than originally planned, she had to purchase more clothes down in the boutique. Thankfully, she kept the bags, which makes it convenient to pack the additional clothing that doesn't fit in the other luggage.

It doesn't take long to gather everything that belongs to her, and a fresh wave of sorrow slams into me. It's getting harder to breathe in here, but now isn't the time to open the sliding glass door for a little fresh air.

"I think that's everything," she states, her eyes scanning the room one final time before landing on me.

More tears swim in those deep blue eyes. Every time I look at the ocean, I'll think of them. "All right. I can help you take it all down," I insist, leaving no room for argument.

She nods, turning to grab one of the large shopping bags, but stops, turns, and faces me once more. "Decker, I need you to know, this week…" She swallows hard. "It has been the greatest week of my life."

I smile and pull her into my arms, needing to hold her, even if it's the last time. "Me too, sweetheart." With a deep sigh, I add, "I'm going to miss you."

A sniffle fills the room, and that one little sound completely undoes me. My heart feels ripped to shreds. It will never be whole again.

Gripping my arms, she gazes up. The sadness almost has me begging her to stay, but I know I can't. It's not my place. If she wanted more, she would tell me. "I'm going to miss you too. Thank you, for everything."

"You're very welcome," I reply, needing to say something else before she goes. I run my thumb over her cheek, wiping away wetness, and slip my fingers into her hair. Her familiar scent hits me square in the gut as I lean in and brush my lips across hers. "If, at any point, you're ready to leave, you have a place to stay with me. For a day, a week, or longer"—*Forever would be nice*—"my door is always open for you. Always."

The corners of her mouth curl upward. "Thank you."

Finally, I steal one last kiss, needing to taste her more than I need air. The kiss starts gentle, but the moment I coax her mouth open with my tongue, it turns heated. Just like every kiss we've shared. I can't get enough of her taste and the way she responds. Adeline throws her arms over my shoulders and presses her body against mine. She rubs my fresh tattoo, but I don't give a shit. The pain is real. It reminds me I'm alive.

Before my hands have a chance to wander her body, I slow the kiss and suck in gulps of oxygen. "Kissing you is my favorite," I whisper.

I feel her grin against my mouth as she murmurs, "Being kissed by you is my favorite too."

Then, I do exactly what I don't want to do. I pull back, breaking contact. "Your dad is waiting."

She exhales and nods harshly, already fighting the tears. "Yes."

"Come on, Addi. Let's get you on the road so you're home before it gets too late," I state, reaching for the larger suitcase. Then, realization hits me, and I have my phone out of my pocket, typing in my code. "Turn on your phone."

She moves to the desk and retrieves the device, the one that's been sitting right there, off, most of the trip. Within a few seconds, it's powered on. I pull up my photos and start clicking. Since I'm connected to the Wi-Fi, I pull up the AirDrop feature on my phone and wait for it to find her device. One number comes up.

"Is this you?"

She glances at my screen. "Yes."

Nodding, I click send, waiting for it to move copies of all the photos of our time together to her phone. Before I can tell myself not to, I go back to the AirDrop feature and screenshot the number. I may never use it, but I don't want to walk away without at least having a way to reach her if needed.

"I got them," she replies softly.

"Look at them later," I suggest, knowing her father is more than likely getting impatient. Not that I care. Personally, I don't like the guy, so leaving him hanging for a bit doesn't bother me at all, but the thought of him taking out his irritation on Adeline doesn't sit well with me. The last thing I want to do is cause her more pain, so I slip my phone back in my pocket and grab her bags.

She puts her sandals back on, while I shove on my socks and shoes. Adeline retrieves the smaller of the two suitcases, and with my right hand, I grab the other bags and suitcase handle. Then, we make our way to the door and step out into the hall. The door closes with one final, loud click.

Taking her hand, I lead her to the elevator. We're both silent as it descends and deposits us on the ground floor one last time. We make our way to the front counter, where, fortunately, no guests wait to check in. I know Adeline's eyes are a bit swollen, her makeup a bit smudged, and the thought of people staring at her because she's clearly been crying makes me a little crazy. I still think she's the most beautiful woman I've ever seen.

"Checking out," Adeline says confidently, placing her keycard on the counter.

"I hope you enjoyed your stay," the clerk says, tapping on the keyboard.

Adeline glances my way. "I did. Very much."

The woman prints the receipt and slides it across the counter. "Thank you for staying with us. We hope to see you again soon."

Adeline nods, folding the sheet of paper and slipping it inside her tiny purse. "Thank you."

I can't help but notice she doesn't comment on the possibility of staying here again. Just one more nail in my coffin, a confirmation she doesn't plan to ever return.

The air is still warm as the sun starts to drop, and the moment we step outside, it feels like a completely different beach than the one we just walked on a short time ago. This beach now feels solemn and lonely as we bypass the walkway that leads to the shore and follow the one angled toward the parking lot.

I instantly spot the fancy town car in one of the front parking spots and know it's her father's car. I can see him sitting in the back seat, talking on the phone, and making no move to exit the vehicle to help his daughter.

That's fine. I've got her.

The driver steps out after popping the trunk. "Good day, Miss Montgomery," he greets with a pleasant smile the moment he sees her.

"Hello, George."

"Let me get your things stowed away, and we'll be on the road momentarily," he states as he takes her smaller suitcase and places it inside the trunk.

I hand over the larger piece of luggage, followed by her shopping bags. Then, I turn to face the woman I love, preparing to say goodbye.

"You are the strongest, most beautiful badass I've ever known, Adeline. When I think back on this week, I'll do it with a smile. Remember, my door is always open for you. Go. Find your happiness, sweet Addi. Be free."

She throws her arms around me and clings to my shirt, her head nestling against my neck like a puzzle piece. When she pulls back, she opens her mouth as if to say something, but snaps it closed. Whatever she was about to say dies completely when the back window opens, and her father's head pokes out. "Time to go."

Adeline places her hands against my chest, her fingers gently laying on top of my tattoo. She bends down and places a kiss over the spot I marked just for her. Then, she quickly goes up on her tiptoes and presses the softest, sweetest kiss to my lips. Before I can react, she pulls away and practically runs to the back passenger door, where George is waiting. She doesn't look back, just slips inside and lets the door close gently behind her.

I stand here, watching as they back out of the parking spot and drive away. My heart feels mangled, worse than it did when I received word that my grandfather passed away. This time, I'm watching my love drive away. In a week, I managed to go from no-strings sex to falling in love with a woman I can't have.

Someone who was never mine to begin with.

The sudden rush of loneliness has never felt so suffocating.

"Come sit with me," Marian instructs after I return the mower to her storage shed behind the garage. It's been more than two weeks since Adeline left, and the return to normal just isn't working for me.

I want to tell her I can't, that I have stuff to do, but she's well aware I don't work tonight. The only time I leave my house is to go to the resort—which is hell, by the way, since being there makes me think of her—or to grab food. I've become a frequent flier of fast food lately, mostly because I don't have any desire to grab groceries and cook, nor do I want to go to the diner and risk Yvonne giving me the third degree for being a miserable sack of shit.

Marian stops behind one of the empty seats. "Sit."

I do as instructed, mostly because I don't have the energy to argue. On top of eating like crap for two weeks, I'm not sleeping much either. When I am finally able to pass out from exhaustion, my dreams are filled with images of Adeline. It's both heaven and hell, because I wake up missing the hell out of her with a hard-on that won't go away.

"Lemonade?" she asks, taking the seat beside me and opening the plastic container of fresh, warm peach cinnamon rolls, making my stomach growl loudly. "I thought you might be a bit hungry," she adds with a grin.

I devour a large pastry while she's pouring a glass of lemonade, but she doesn't say a word. She just grabs a second one and places it on my plate before retrieving one for herself and taking a small bite.

"Have you talked to her?" she asks when I'm halfway through my second roll.

I contemplate acting ignorant, but I know that won't work. Marian knows me better than almost anyone else, with the exception of Todd, so playing dumb won't get me very far with her. "No."

She seems positively dumbfounded. "Why?"

I shrug and decide honesty is the only way to go. "Because we were temporary, Marian. We knew we were only spending a week together."

She scoffs and waves her hand at the thought. "That's hogwash, Decker Paulson. I saw your face and how you acted. I most definitely can see how miserable you are right now."

I shove the rest of my second roll into my mouth and mumble, "I'm not miserable."

Marian laughs. Actually laughs hard in my face, as if what I said—or tried to say, considering my mouth was full of food—was the funniest joke she ever heard. "Oh, silly, silly boy. You are most definitely miserable. And heartbroken," she says, sipping her lemonade. "So, what are you going to do about it?"

When I finally swallow the food turning sour in my stomach, I lean back in my chair and cross my arms over my chest. "Nothing."

Her mouth slowly falls open as she gapes at me. "Decker Michael Paulson, you are the stupidest boy I've ever met, and I've met some pretty dumb ones in my lifetime."

The corner of my lip turns upward. "It's not Michael."

"Allen? Jeffery? Richard?"

I shake my head no, loving the sense of normal I feel when I'm around her.

"I'm surprised. You've been acting a bit like a Richard," she mumbles softly, yet loud enough for me to hear.

"What?" I ask, gaping in shock.

Marian rolls her eyes at me. "Oh, don't act like you haven't been. You're moping around here, all sad and depressed, when all you really have to do is go after the girl."

I rub my forehead at the place my headache is quickly forming. "It's not that simple."

She hits her hand on the table, making the contents on top jump and clang. "Love is never simple, Decker. You have to fight for it, every day."

"She made the decision to go home," I argue, wishing I would have gone into my rental house and bypassed the lemonade and cinnamon rolls.

"Did you give her a reason to stay?" she asks, her eyes full of concern.

Sighing, I close my eyes and instantly picture her face. "No. I offered to drive her home, but she didn't want that."

"But did you ask her to stay? Did you say, *Adeline, I love you. Stay with me. Marry me and give me babies so Marian can spoil them rotten for the rest of her life?* Did you?"

I can't help but laugh. That simple action causes the tightness in my chest to ease, even just for a single second. "No, can't say I said those exact words."

She waves her hand. "Well, maybe not those exact words, silly, but the concept is the same."

After a few long seconds, my mouth opens and words fly out, all on their own, without instruction from my brain. "I wasn't planning on falling in love with her, but I did. I think she felt the same, but it was hard to tell. We both keep a shield around our hearts so we can protect ourselves from the assholes who are supposed to love us unconditionally, but only know how to make demands."

"Speaking of assholes, have you talked to your father?"

I shake my head. Marian is one of the only people who know about my past. It took time before I did, but it's hard not to trust the crazy ol' woman when she's so caring and loving to me.

"Maybe you should. Maybe it's time to put that whole mess behind you. Perhaps, you'd be truly able to fight for your future if you weren't constantly looking over your shoulder."

Her words are a direct hit on their target, and she knows it.

Scrubbing my hands over my face, I give her my complete attention. "He wants the money. He knows I don't want it, but I'm not giving it to him." It's not because I need it, or use it for that matter. My grandfather told me not to give my father a cent. Made me promise, actually, and there's no way I'll ever break a promise to him.

"As you shouldn't. Your grandfather, rest his soul, left it to you for a reason. He left his company to your father. It's not anyone's fault but your dad's that the company is doing so poorly and could use an influx of cash to keep it afloat."

My right eyebrow moves skyward. "How do you know that?"

She shrugs and pours a little more lemonade into her glass. "I've read up on it. It's not every day one of my dear friends is a descendant to one of the world's biggest software companies in the world."

I crack a smile. "It's not the biggest, but it's one of the oldest," I remind her. My grandfather was an accounting genius and invented one of the first software systems used in accounting firms across the United States in the seventies. The company took off and grew over the years, thanks to my grandfather's leadership and direction as CEO of the company. When he retired a few years before he died, my father—his only son—took over and has slowly run it into the ground.

"You need to deal with your past, Decker."

Sighing, I nod, knowing she's right. I need to deal with my father once and for all, so the constant contact and threats stop.

"Deal with your father, and then go get the girl. She loves you, you know." My eyes fly up to the familiar ones at the table beside me. "Oh, don't act so surprised. You might be a little dense sometimes, but you're a very loveable man, Decker Paulson."

For the first time since Adeline left, a big smile spreads across my face. Not a fake one or a little one. A full-wattage grin that makes my cheeks hurt. "You really think she does?" I ask, finding this wave of uncertainty very uncomfortable. I've never been hesitant or lacked confidence, so to feel it is a bit unsettling.

"Of course she does. It was written all over her face," Marian assures me.

"That was the delicious cinnamon rolls you served her," I quip, reaching over and squeezing her hand.

She beams back at me. "Those were a distant second to how she feels about you."

We sit in silence for several minutes, both of us lost in our own thoughts as we enjoy the gorgeous midmorning Tuesday. Her words keep playing through my mind, and it doesn't take long before I realize she's right. I need to deal with my father face-to-face so I can finally let my past go and move on. I don't want the company. Never did.

I want Adeline.

Or at least the opportunity to see where our undeniable chemistry goes.

Maybe it won't lead us anywhere.

Or perhaps it'll take us straight to forever.

Chapter
TWENTY ONE

Adeline

The office is silent as I wrap up the research my father required I complete before I could go home. That's fine though. I prefer the quiet of the floor, especially since I don't have a real office of my own to close out the rest of the world.

When I arrived back in Charleston three weeks ago, I did as I was told. I met with the partners, my father included, and apologized for the email I sent criticizing the appointment of my colleague and the good ol' boy men's club that runs the business. At my father's insistence, I played it off as severe stress due to the cases I was assisting with and my time away for my friend's wedding, which didn't happen and created additional pressure in my life. I received a disciplinary review in my employment file but didn't lose my job. They made sure to tell me the only reason I was still here was because of my father.

Too bad, I wish I had been fired.

Since then, I have been unofficially demoted to researcher with the paralegals. I'm not even sitting in on client meetings or offered any smaller cases, despite being a lawyer who is more than capable. I'm basically out of sight, out of mind, and it just confirms the fact I *don't* want to do this job for the rest of my life.

I barely want to do it for the next week.

But the plus side to keeping busy like this is there's no time to dwell on my heartache over losing Decker. My father hasn't mentioned him since we left the resort, which I suppose is a positive. That means he's already moved on from his diabolical attempt to ruin his life. At least I hope that's what it means, because as long as Decker is no longer in my father's crosshairs, I can live with this constant pain in my chest. He's still free.

I gather up the papers I've completed and turn to head for the copy room. I've learned to always keep electronic and paper copies of my research, mostly to cover my own butt. Some people lose it. Others use it as if it were their own, and there's nothing worse than someone else taking credit for your work.

Once I have copies sent to my email from the copier, I gather it up and head to my father's office. He had a dinner meeting earlier, which is why I was working late. He wanted to review my work over the weekend before a big client conference on Monday morning.

Making my way through the maze of hallways, I reach the back one that houses the partners. The hall itself is wider, the doors grander, and the views from inside the offices spectacular. Ensuring my work is secure inside a legal folder, I approach his half-closed door, only to stop in my tracks when I hear voices.

"I think this case is perfect for Adeline," a voice from a phone says. I instantly recognize it as William Ward, one of the three partners.

"No, absolutely not," my father says.

There's a long pause. "I understand you're still upset at her—" Mr. Ward starts but is cut off.

"Adeline isn't big case material. She's fine doing all the research for us, but I don't want her serving clients in this capacity," my father states, making my heart clench in my chest. "Besides, she won't be with us long enough to succeed. Jefferson Martin plans to propose later this fall, and that'll be the end of her working. She'll be a good little wife, taking care of his home, while he grows a successful political career, like his father."

"All right. We'll give the case to Ethan Hatherley. He's really proving to be an asset and is willing to put in the time to be successful," Mr. Ward says.

Bile rises in my throat as I think about Ethan's *work*. Most of the research he passes off as his is mine, and the only time this man puts into his work is before his extended lunches.

"Sounds good. We can assign Adeline to his research and documentation. She's good at making copies."

A silent tear falls down my cheek as his words register. A confirmation, if you will, that I'll never be more than a disposable pawn in my father's game of life. As long as he has power over all the pieces, he's in complete control over the game, and now I know exactly where I stand.

I'll never be an equal.

I'll never be someone he can be proud of.

The truth is looking me square in the eye, showing me his true colors.

He'll never love me, not the way a father should love a daughter.

Like a bucket of cold water, realization hits me hard and painful. If I stay, I will never have the life I want. I will be forced into the one cherry-picked by someone else, forced into a loveless marriage for the sake of duty and honor. That's no way to live.

Not the way I want to live.

"Schedule the meeting with Ethan on Monday morning," my father states to his partner and friend.

"Will do. What about Adeline?"

"I'll take care of her. She'll be attending that Save the Ocean Life Gala fundraiser tomorrow night with Jefferson. I'll mention to her that she's being assigned to assist Ethan. She won't say a word while in the presence of dignitaries. She's been trained better than that."

Anger flows through my veins as they wrap up their conversation and sign off. My feet are moving before I can even consider what course of action would be appropriate. Instead, I storm into his office, causing him to jump in his seat at his office door smacking against the wall.

"A-adeline," he stammers, standing up from behind his massive desk. "What is the meaning of this?"

A wave of calm washes over me as I look at the man before me. The one I've spent my entire life trying to please, to always show him who I really am. But that never mattered. He is never going to see the real me, or even let me find out who that person is, and I can't live like that. I won't.

Not anymore.

"I'm done," I answer coolly and confidently.

"What? With the research?"

"No. I'm done with you. I'm done working here. I'm done being your pawn."

His ears and cheeks turn red as he steels his spine and glares across the desk at me. "This is outrageous, young lady. You have no right to speak to me this way," he demands, but I refuse to let him finish.

"No right? Are you kidding me? *You* have no right to treat me this way. All I've ever wanted was to make you proud of me. I was Valedictorian in high school and earned the top spot in law school."

He scoffs and rolls his eyes. "You earned nothing, daughter. You received that top spot because of me. Your name and my money got you where you were."

My throat goes dry and the tears well up in my eyes. "You paid?"

"Of course I paid to get you there. It's not like you could have achieved those grades on your own," he spits at me, the poisonous words hitting their mark.

But I know the truth. I worked my ass off through law school, got the grades I received because of *my* valor. I was at the top of my class because of me, not him. I don't care how much money he threw at them. It'll never take away what I did while I was enrolled there, nor the determination and drive it took to achieve it.

I'm proud of my hard work, even if my own father isn't.

I take in the man before me. The bitter, heartless soul who raised me, even though he has no right to ever claim he did. There's no real love there, and my entire life, that's all I really wanted.

That's when Decker fills my mind. I see his face, the way his eyes lit up every time he saw me. I recall the way he held my hand and kissed my lips. I think back to every experience he gave me, every moment we shared. Even the simple ones such as snuggling in the early morning hours were magical.

They were real.

Ours.

"I want Decker," I whisper, as if finally vocalizing what my heart has been telling me since I met the sexy guy who works at the resort.

My father's eyes narrow. "The bartender? Are you kidding me? I've arranged for you to marry the governor's son, for Christ's sake!" he bellows.

"No."

"Stop being a spoiled brat," he begins, but I won't let him continue.

"I love Decker. I don't care about what he does or what his last name is. All I know is how he makes me feel. I love him, and I'm pretty sure he loves me too," I say, stepping forward and dropping the folder onto his desk.

"He does."

Spinning around, I come face-to-face with the man I've fallen helplessly and utterly in love with. A smile spreads across my lips as I take in his jeans and button-down. His brown eyes are tired and his jaw is scruffy, as if he hasn't shaved in a while, but other than that, he's the same Decker I fell for weeks ago.

"How in the hell did you get in here?" my father yells behind me, but we both ignore him.

"You're a sight for sore eyes," I say, giving him my complete attention and taking a few steps in his direction.

"Likewise," he replies, his lips soft and slightly curling up.

"What are you doing here?" I ask, my heart trying to beat right out of my chest.

"I came for you."

I almost run into his arms right here and now but force myself to hold my position. "Me?"

He nods and takes a step toward me. "Yes, you. I came to ask you something."

"Oh?"

Another step closer. "I was wondering if you'd go out with me?" he asks with that touch of cocky confidence I fell in love with.

"I'd love to," I quickly reply. "When?"

He glances down at his watch. "What are you doing right now?"

Smiling, I tell him, "Nothing. Turns out, I'm going to have a lot of free time for a while. I no longer have a job."

"Or a home!" my father bellows angrily. "If you walk out that door, consider yourself cut off."

I spin around and confidently face Edward Montgomery, my head held high. Decker is there beside me, taking my hand and giving it a gentle squeeze in support. "I don't need your money."

My father laughs. "Of course you do. You think you can build a life with this…this criminal? You know nothing about him!"

Decker politely turns me so I'm facing him. "You know me better than anyone, and what you don't know, we'll learn together along the way. You know I was best friends with my grandfather. Well, he started a company in the seventies after creating one of the first accounting software systems. He brought his son into the fold, and yes, was hoping his grandson too someday.

"However, he realized I didn't want to help run the company, so as he aged, he made arrangements to leave the company to my dad and set up a trust for me."

"Another worthless man skipping out on his responsibilities to his family," my dad interrupts.

Decker isn't fazed, however. He just holds my gaze and says, "I'm hardly worthless. My trust is more than enough to live comfortably on." He winks and gives that confident smirk. "Anyway, my father tried to bully me into working for his company, taking legal action against me to try to force my hand. He's tried everything he could to get his hands on my trust fund, because the company has been slowly sinking and he needs the cash."

"Oh," I reply, understanding what it's like to be betrayed by someone who's supposed to love you.

"Also, I believe what Edward meant when he called me a criminal was an indecent exposure charge from college. I was with friends leaving a bar late one night and had to pee. Apparently, you can be charged with indecent exposure if you pee in public, including an unused alleyway. They ended up dropping the charges."

I can't help but smile. "Ruthless criminal," I quip, earning a smile in return.

"Most definitely. And to clear up any confusion on my father, I actually just left there. We had a very lengthy discussion about the company and my lack of involvement in it. I presented him with an opportunity. I offered to purchase my grandfather's old cabin. In exchange, I would pay him five times the appraisal value, and he will never ask me for money or try to take legal action against me again. I'm happy to say, he signed."

"Really? That's great," I tell him, stepping forward and throwing my arms around his shoulders. I go to kiss him, but he pulls back, meeting my gaze.

"It is. So, what do you say, Adeline? Wanna go to North Carolina with me and check out my new cabin?"

I'm already nodding. "Yes."

"We'll have to be back in Florida by Tuesday, because I'm scheduled to work, but after that, we can decide where we want to go. It can be anywhere in the world, sweetheart."

"What if we stay in Florida for a while? I think I'd like to get to know Marian more," I tell him excitedly.

"Done," he replies, taking my hand and leading me to the door of my father's office.

"And when we have some free time, you can teach me how to fish at your new cabin," I suggest, already loving the sound of long weekends away at Decker's favorite spot.

"Most definitely," Decker replies as we get ready to breach the threshold.

"Where do you think you're going?" my father demands from behind me.

I pause and glance over my shoulder. "Florida. Well, first North Carolina."

He seems positively exasperated. "If you walk out that door, you're done. You won't get one single red cent from me!"

I shrug, realizing I don't want or need his money. All I ever wanted was his support and love, but since that's not on the table, I'm more than ready to walk away, sadly. "I don't want it."

His laughter lacks humor. "What are you going to do? Live off Decker's trust fund?"

Glancing at Decker over my shoulder, I casually say, "Yeah. Or I'll open my own boutique. Or maybe I'll take the bar in Florida and open my own practice? Who knows, but whatever I do will be my decision."

"And I'll support it," Decker replies proudly before adding, "And I'll support her, because I love her."

My father sneers in disgust. "I no longer have a daughter."

Turning, I face him head-on. "And that's your decision, sadly. You only want a daughter under your terms and conditions, and unfortunately, you'll be the one missing out on any relationship that could have been. This was your choice. While you're here, dictating every aspect of your life and the people in it, I'll be happy and loved. I'll be free."

I feel Decker squeeze my hand as we turn back to the door and step through it. We continue to walk through the massive hallway, past the cubicles and conference rooms and back to my tiny closet I call an office. I grab my purse from my locked drawer and open the middle drawer to grab the only personal item I will be taking with me.

"You printed it?" he asks, looking over my shoulder at the photograph in my hand. It's from our helicopter tour that last day I was in Florida.

"Yes."

He smiles and slips the photo into the pocket of his button-down. "What else?"

"Nothing. I'm not taking anything with me."

Decker takes my hand and leads me from my office and toward the elevator. We don't speak. We ride down in silence, our fingers entwined. When the car deposits us onto the ground floor, he guides me toward the front entrance, where Eric, the security guard, waits. "I see you found Miss Montgomery."

"I did. Thank you for your assistance, Eric. If you're ever in Florida, give me a call. We'd be happy to meet you for dinner."

Eric smiles widely. "I may take you up on that, Decker." He nods at me. "Enjoy your evening, ma'am."

We step through the front entrance and onto the sidewalk outside. "What…"

"I'll explain in the car."

Nodding in agreement, we walk to the parking lot and toward an unfamiliar waiting car.

Decker stops and turns, bringing my hand to his lips and placing a tender kiss on my knuckles. "Ready to blow this Popsicle stand?"

I'm already grinning. "I'm ready."

Chapter
TWENTY TWO

Decker

The moment we're inside the car, all I can do is smile. She's even more beautiful than I expected when I stepped onto her floor and went in search of the woman I love.

"You're here."

"I am," I tell her, holding her hands in my own as we both swivel in our seats to face each other.

"How? When? Where?" she mutters, as if trying to wrap her head around what has happened in the last thirty minutes.

"I'll start at the beginning," I tell her after turning over the car and making sure the temperature is comfortable. "My father wasn't always a selfish man, but as money and power were so readily available and he was sitting at the helm of a multi-million-dollar company, he changed. He insisted I work with him because it was my destiny, but my grandfather understood it wasn't. My father manipulated the situation, using guilt as a weapon for years, and when I was finally free, it was because my grandfather helped me.

"When Marian was reading me the riot act earlier this week, telling me in no uncertain terms to get my head out of my ass, I realized what I want. You. Or at least the opportunity to try, but she also reminded me I have to deal with the bullshit in my past before I can completely focus on my future.

"So, I went to Norfolk to see my father. He has desperately wanted the money left to me, but thanks to my grandfather's lawyers, the trust was ironclad. He couldn't get his hands on it. I also made the old man a promise I'd never give it to him, so I had to come up with a way to get him off my ass for good. That's when I remembered he received the cabin in the will. My best childhood memories are with my grandpa at that cabin, fishing and cooking our catch over the open fire, and I realized I had an opportunity. I offered him five million for the property, and in order to get the money, he'd sign over the deed and promise to never come after me for more money again."

"And he took it," she confirms.

I nod.

"Wait. You bought a cabin for five million dollars? And paid five times the appraisal price? How big is this cabin?"

A smile spreads across my lips. "Not very big. A thousand square feet, maybe? But it's in the middle of a hundred-acre timbered property with a private lake in front of it."

Her eyes widen comically. "Seriously?"

"Seriously," I reply, running my finger across her knuckles. "He signed last night, so today we went to the bank and title company to have everything taken care of. As soon as it was settled, I jumped in a rental car and drove down here to you."

"I'm so glad you did," she whispers, bringing my hand to her lips and kissing my thumb. "My father has been awful. He threatened to destroy you. That's why I left with him."

My heart thunders in my chest. If it were possible to hate Edward Montgomery more, it was accomplished with that one statement. "He made you choose him."

She nods solemnly. "To protect you."

"You don't ever have to protect me again, Addi. Not like that. If there's something you need to know or you're afraid, you come to me. We'll figure it out together."

"I realized that when I was standing in the hallway, listening to him spew garbage about me. I was always going to be under his control and was never going to be happy."

"I'm proud of you," I tell her, cupping her cheek with my palm. Her skin is so soft and smooth, so exactly how I remember it. Granted, it's only been a few weeks since I've touched her, but those weeks were the worst kind of torture.

"I was coming for you," she adds.

"Good. Because we deserve the opportunity to see where this leads."

"I know where I'm hoping it goes," she says softly, and even though it's dark inside my car except for the glow of the interior dash lights, I can tell she's blushing.

"Yeah? Where's that?"

"Somewhere we can get naked."

A bark of laughter slides easily from my lips. "Your wish is my command, Miss Montgomery."

"Decker?" she asks, and I swear she leans a little closer as she says my name.

"Yes, love?"

"Will you kiss me now?"

I'm smiling widely as I start to close the distance between us. "There's nothing I want more in this world."

Pressing my lips against hers, I feel a rightness in my soul for the first time in weeks. All the unhappiness, stress, and fear just falls away, leaving only her and me. She tilts her head just a touch, granting me better access to devour her sweet mouth. My tongue slides against hers, tasting and savoring. Her lips are as sweet as honey, and I can't get enough of them.

Suddenly, she rips her mouth from my own and sucks in a deep breath. "Wait. Eric."

My eyebrows draw together in confusion. "You're thinking of another dude right now? While I'm kissing you?" I tease.

"No...well, yes, but only because I need to know how you knew him."

"Believe it or not, I went to school with Eric."

She stares at me with a blank look on her face. "Seriously?"

"Yeah, small world, isn't it? I had no idea he worked there until I walked in. Well, technically, I had to call inside and be buzzed in, but when we realized we knew each other, it was pretty easy to gain access. I told him why I was there, to get my girl, and he gave me directions to your floor."

She smiles, but it quickly vanishes. "He's probably going to be fired. For breaking protocol and buzzing you up."

"Apparently, he's prepared for that. Insisted he'd be fine and not to worry about it if it happens. He informed me there's always a security job available around the city."

She shakes her head, as if she can't quite believe it. Honestly, I'm not so sure I believe the coincidence myself. I was prepared for something drastic like paying the guy off or maybe a little B&E to gain access, but, thankfully, that was completely unnecessary. Not that I know anything about breaking and entering, but it was the principle. I was ready to do anything to get to the woman I love.

Speaking of…

"I love you," I blurt out. "I don't exactly know when it happened, but it did. Sometime during our week together, I fell helplessly in love with you. I know we're still new and we can take this relationship as slow as you want, but—"

"I love you too. For the first time in my life, I'm ready to take the risk. I want to jump off the cliff without knowing what's below," she states.

Sliding my thumb across the apple of her cheek, I tell her, "I'll catch you. You jump, I'm there." When she smiles, I instruct, "Say it again."

"I love you too."

My mouth is on hers a second later, trying to convey exactly how much she means to me. It's easy to do when she has quickly become my entire world, the woman I didn't even realize I dreamed about until she was standing before me.

I'm not sure how long we sit here and make out like two teenagers, but eventually, we both come up for air. "Wow," she mutters, licking her swollen lips. Her eyes are glazed over as she looks my way.

"I have that effect on women," I joke, giving her a cocky grin.

She chuckles and slides her hand up the inseam of my jeans. I know exactly where it's headed, and my cock couldn't be happier. "Hopefully not all women."

My eyes cross and a groan seeps from my lips as she cups my erection and squeezes her hand against it. "There's only one woman who matters," I assure her. "Ready?"

"Yes," she replies, as I pull from the parking lot.

"Your place?" I ask, turning in the direction I know her building is located. She wasn't there when I stopped by earlier, which is why I ended up at her office. It was my second choice for finding her.

"Yes, though it won't be mine for long."

"That's okay," I tell her. "We'll grab your personal things and go to a hotel for the night."

"Sounds perfect," she replies, slipping her hand inside of mine. "I'm rather fond of inviting you up to my hotel room."

I chuckle low and gravelly. "That was a pretty incredible night."

"It was."

"What do you say we skip going to your condo and I just take you back to my hotel and make love to you all night long?"

"I say I can replace anything in my condo I may be unable to retrieve," she states. I'm assuming because she doesn't know what her father will do. He could very easily have her banned from her own residence, refusing to let her collect any of her belongings inside.

"We'll go shopping," I insist.

Adeline shrugs her shoulders. "It'll all work out, Decker. I'm not going to worry about it."

So, we don't. In the short drive to the hotel, she tells me all about her phone calls with Reece, who she's remained in close contact with for the last three weeks, and about the prospect of visiting Kentucky where Reece and her family live. By the time we park and head into the hotel, it's as if no time has passed at all. We're two people, madly in love, and ready to take the next step in life together.

It's not as scary as I thought it'd be.

Instead, it's quite the opposite.

I feel calm.

Settled.

I can't imagine not having her in my life, by my side, and I get a secret thrill knowing we've got as much time as we want or need to figure the rest of it out. For now, we'll take it day by day, or in this case, night by night.

And tonight, I'm going to show her exactly how much I love her.

With my body.

Something tells me we're both in for a long, wild night.

I can't wait.

Epilogue

Adeline

December

"I'm a little worried about Marian. Maybe we should go back and check on her," I insist as we walk along one of the well-maintained paths through the timber. This particular one leads toward the lake, where we've spent the last two days fishing and relaxing in Adirondack chairs.

"She's fine, Addi. You know Marian. After we played Scrabble she wanted to go to the guest room with her tea and get ready for bed," he says, giving my hand a gentle squeeze.

The moon is high in the sky above the trees, lighting the walkway in front of us. The late-December North Carolina air is cool and perfect for a sweater.

This entire trip has been amazing. We've spent at least one long weekend a month at the cabin, slowly updating it, inside and out. Apparently, Decker's father never used it, and it slowly started to rot away without anyone checking on it or keeping it maintained. He considered hiring someone to do the work, but ultimately decided to do as much of it as he could. He felt like his grandfather would have wanted that, and if he were alive, would have been right beside him, helping.

After five months of working on it, the cabin is completely updated. It's still rustic and cozy, but now has all the amenities you could want, including air-conditioning for the summer, new appliances, and a second bathroom. Decker's grandfather's old stuffed fish are still on the walls, and his rocking chair on the front porch. It's as if he's still a part of our trips here, even though it's in spirit.

"I'm so glad she came with us. It wouldn't have been Christmas without her," I state as we approach the clearing.

"I agree. It helped sway her decision, since she's not flying out to visit her son and his family until New Year's Eve."

We break through the tree line and onto the grassy shore by the lake. It's so peaceful and serene here. I never really pictured myself as a lake and cabin girl, but I've quickly discovered there's no other place I'd rather be. Well, except in Decker's arms. That's my favorite spot. But besides our little home in Florida, this property is a very close second.

"Come on, let's walk for a few minutes," he suggests, guiding me toward the water's edge. We stay on the grass, the sound of crickets chirping and an owl calling filling the night.

"Do you think Marian liked her monthly gardening subscription?" I ask, still worrying that she didn't like one of her Christmas gifts.

"You saw her face. She loved it," he reassures me. The yearly subscription includes a monthly magazine, as well as plants and flowers to be delivered every four weeks. When I saw it online, I knew it would be right up her alley, and I am so pleased she really liked it.

"What did you think about yours?" I ask, glancing up and watching his entire face transform with happiness.

"Are you kidding me? You couldn't tell how much I loved it by how I reacted?" he asks.

I could tell. The moment he opened the canvas portrait, his eyes filled with tears. It was an old image I found tucked away at the cabin of grandfather and grandson fishing along the lake. They're both smiling, looking at each other with their lines in the water and their feet buried in the mud. He told me his grandmother took the picture, and unbeknownst to me, had it framed and hanging in the family room at their home in Norfolk. He never knew what happened to the picture after his grandpa passed away and was thrilled and relieved to see it again.

He stops and turns to face me, his hands sliding up my arms. "Did you like yours?"

I shake my head, still trying to wrap it around the fact I'm now a property owner. "I still can't believe it."

"Believe it, baby." He presses his lips to my forehead. "I'm so proud of you, and now you have a spot to open your own boutique."

It still seems so surreal. Decker purchased an ocean front shop just up the beach from some of our favorite hangouts and is giving me free rein to transform the space into the boutique of my dreams. I have a whole binder of ideas for design and merchandise, and now I can't believe I'll be able to put some of those possibilities into action.

"Best Christmas gift ever," I reassure him.

He grins widely. "You know what we should do? We should look for shells."

Confusion mars my features, I'm sure. "Shells? In the lake?"

He shrugs. "Yeah, why not?"

Skeptically, I watch as he looks down, scouring the earth for shells. Personally, I think he's a little nuts, but if he wants to look for seashells —at night—I suppose that's what we'll do. It only takes a few seconds before I spot something lying at the edge of the grass. I release his hand and bend down to check out what I assume is a rock. However, upon closer inspection, I see it's actually a shell. And not just any shell either.

A Junonia shell that looks very familiar.

Before I can stand up, something pokes me in the finger. I turn the shell around and find something sticking out of the back of it. I'm about to drop the shell as images of spiders and crabs fill my mind, but then something catches the moonlight just perfectly and sparkles. I bring the shell up close and realize it's a ring.

Confused, I stand up, holding the shell and ring. "Decker, there's a ring in this—" I stop talking the moment I find him on one knee in front of me. "Holy shit," I whisper, gaping at the man I love.

He grins. "You never curse."

Clearing my throat, I mutter, "Well, this seemed like an S-bomb kind of moment."

His smile spreads. "A good kinda moment?" he asks hopefully.

"Well, that depends on the question. If you're just bending down tying your shoe, then it might not be S-bomb worthy," I reply, my mouth so dry I don't know how I can get words out.

"I'm not wearing tie shoes," he quips, having stuffed his feet into a pair of comfortable slip-ons when we decided to go for a walk. "And yes, I do have a question for you."

"Okay," I mutter, gripping the shell in my hand so tightly the ring is leaving an indentation in my palm.

He gingerly pries my fingers apart and exposes the shell, taking it from my hand and removing the ring. It looks like he used some sort of putty to keep it in place, which I'm a tad bit grateful for. The way my hands are shaking, I'm sure I would have dropped it in the dirt.

"You know, I had this entire speech planned out. I knew what I wanted to say, but now that we're here, the only thing that seems necessary is to tell you I love you. That I want to spend the rest of my life with you. Marry me, Addi."

Tears slide down my cheeks as I nod. "Yes. Yes, I'll marry you."

He stands up and has me in his arms in a flash, pressing his mouth to mine and sealing our agreement with a kiss. "I love you," he whispers, sliding the solitaire diamond onto my ring finger. He brings it to his mouth and kisses my knuckle. "Thank you for making me the happiest I've ever been."

"I love you too," I say, throwing my arms around his neck and pressing my chest against his.

His mouth is hot and familiar as he coaxes my lips apart and devours me with his tongue. I'll never get enough of kissing this man. It's as if we were put on this earth to find each other, and now that we have, life seems to be a little easier. Not perfect by any means, but definitely better than it was before.

"Ready?" he asks, breaking the kiss once more.

"For?" I ask breathlessly.

He just gives me that same cocky grin I fell for all those months ago at the resort. "For the rest of our lives."

"Oh," I reply, taking his proffered hand and smiling like a lunatic. "Definitely."

He escorts me back up to the cabin, where Marian is waiting with champagne and fresh peach cinnamon rolls. How she managed to whip them up in the time we were gone is beyond me, but I'm not going to complain. Enjoying Marian's warm pastries only seems right in the moment.

With my new fiancé at my side and our honorary grandmother in front of us, we toast to love.

To forever.

To the night I kissed a stranger.

The End

Thank you for reading Kissing A Stranger.
Want more of the Kissing Games Series?

Kissing My Brother's Bride
Molly McLain
https://books2read.com/KissingMyBrothersBride

Kissing the Rival
Kaylee Ryan
https://books2read.com/KissingTheRival

Kissing My Crush
C.A. Harms
https://books2read.com/KissingCrush

Kissing A Stranger
Lacey Black
https://books2read.com/KissingAStranger

Kissing My Soulmate
Evan Grace
https://books2read.com/Kissingmy-Soulmate

Don't miss a single reveal, release, or sale! Sign up for my newsletter.
http://www.laceyblackbooks.com/newsletter

More from
LACEY BLACK

Rivers Edge series

Trust Me, Rivers Edge book 1 (Maddox and Avery) – FREE at all retailers

Fight Me, Rivers Edge book 2 (Jake and Erin)

Expect Me, Rivers Edge book 3 (Travis and Josselyn)

Promise Me: A Novella, Rivers Edge book 3.5 (Jase and Holly)

Protect Me, Rivers Edge book 4 (Nate and Lia)

Boss Me, Rivers Edge book 5 (Will and Carmen)

Trust Us: A Rivers Edge Christmas Novella (Maddox and Avery)

~ This novella was originally part of the Christmas Miracles Anthology

BOX SET – contains all 5 novels, 2 novellas, and a BONUS short story

With Me, A Rivers Edge Christmas Novella (Brooklyn and Becker)

Bound Together series

Submerged, Bound Together book 1 (Blake and Carly)

Profited, Bound Together book 2 (Reid and Dani)

Entwined, Bound Together book 3 (Luke and Sidney)

Summer Sisters series

My Kinda Kisses, Summer Sisters book 1 (Jaime and Ryan)

My Kinda Night, Summer Sisters book 2 (Payton and Dean)

My Kinda Song, Summer Sisters book 3 (Abby and Levi)

My Kinda Mess, Summer Sisters book 4 (Lexi and Linkin)

My Kinda Player, Summer Sisters book 5 (AJ and Sawyer)

My Kinda Player, Summer Sisters book 6 (Meghan and Nick)

My Kinda Wedding, A Summer Sisters Novella book 7 (Meghan and Nick)

Rockland Falls series

Love and Pancakes, Rockland Falls book 1

Love and Lingerie, Rockland Falls book 2
Love and Landscape, Rockland Falls book 3
Love and Neckties, Rockland Falls book 4

Standalone
Music Notes, a sexy contemporary romance standalone
A Place To Call Home, a Memorial Day novella
Exes and Ho Ho Ho's, a sexy contemporary romance standalone novella
Pants on Fire, a sexy contemporary romance standalone
Double Dog Dare You, a new standalone
Grip, A Driven World Novel
Bachelor Swap, A Bachelor Tower Series Novel
Perfect Kiss, Mason Creek Series book 9
Waiting For Love, The Love Vixen Series book 11
Quarterback Keeper, a surprise baby novella
Kissing A Stranger, The Kissing Games book 4

Burgers and Brew Crüe Series
Kickstart My Heart
Don't Go Away Mad
Same Ol' Situation
Wild Side
What's It Gonna Take
Home Sweet Home
Too Young to Fall in Love
Without You

Pine Village Series
Pretty Remarkable, a free prequel short story
Pretty Incredible, book 1

Co-Written with *NYT Bestselling* Author, Kaylee Ryan
It's Not Over, Fair Lakes book 1
Just Getting Started, Fair Lakes book 2
Can't Get Enough, Fair Lakes book 3

Fair Lakes Box Set

Boy Trouble

Home To You, a second chance novella

Beneath the Fallen Stars

Tell Me A Story

Royal – Writing as Rebel Shaw

Crying Shame – Writing as Rebel Shaw

ACKNOWLEDGMENTS

Wow, what an amazing project to be a part of! When Molly McLain came to me with her idea for this multi-author series, I was in from the very start, and I couldn't have asked for a better group of authors to join forces with! Thank you, Molly, Kaylee, CA, and Evan for making this series the MOST fun ever and for all the laughs!

Thank you to my editing team – Kara Hildebrand, Sandra Shipman, Joanne Thompson, Julie Deaton, and Karen Hrdlicka. I couldn't do this without you!!

A huge thanks to the book team - Photographer, Wander Aguiar; Model, Lucas Loyola; Cover Designer, Sarah Paige of The Book Cover Boutique; Graphics Designer, MSB Designs; Formatting design by Tami at Integrity Formatting; and Promotions by Give Me Books. Thank you for everything! I work with the best!!

Kaylee Ryan, Lacey's Ladies, Chasidy Renee, Holly Collins, and my ARC team, thank you for constant support and pushing me to be the best I can be!

To my husband and kids, thank you for helping me live my dream.

To all the bloggers and readers, thank you, thank you, thank you. I hope you enjoy this story as much as I loved writing it.

Contact
LACEY BLACK

USA Today Bestselling Author Lacey Black is a Midwestern girl with a passion for reading, writing, and shopping. She carries her e-reader with her everywhere she goes so she never misses an opportunity to read a few pages. Always looking for a happily ever after, Lacey is passionate about contemporary romance novels and enjoys it further when you mix in a little suspense. She resides in a small town in Illinois with her husband, two children, adorable black lab puppy, crazy cat, and three rowdy chickens.

Website: www.laceyblackbooks.com
    Email: laceyblackwrites@gmail.com
    Facebook: https://www.facebook.com/authorlaceyblack
    Instagram: https://www.instagram.com/laceyblackwrites/
    Bookbub: https://www.bookbub.com/authors/lacey-black
    Amazon: https://www.amazon.com/Lacey-Black/e/B00MW2UGZI
    Twitter: https://twitter.com/AuthLaceyBlack
    Goodreads: https://www.goodreads.com/author/show/8414783.Lacey_Black

Sign up for my newsletter so you don't miss a single sale, reveal, or release!
    http://www.laceyblackbooks.com/newsletter

www.ingramcontent.com/pod-product-compliance
Lightning Source LLC
Chambersburg PA
CBHW060642260626
47161CB00008B/2959